Last of the Boy Soldiers

by
John H Oliver

Last of the Boy Soldiers
First Edition
Published by DreamStar Books, January 2005
Lasyard House
Underhill Street
Bridgnorth
Shropshire
WV16 4BB
Tel: 0870 777 3339
e-mail: dreamstar@jakarna.co.uk

ISBN 1 904166 05 9

Typeset in Garamond

Printed and bound in Great Britain by Antony Rowe Ltd

Last of the Boy Soldiers

About the author

Born in Willenhall, West Midlands, the son of the local policeman, John began writing soon after completing his engineering apprenticeship. With over 200 published articles to his name, he has written for BBC television, radio and national newspapers, including The Times and Daily Telegraph. He became a regular features writer for several health and fitness magazines and has been a regular contributor to The Midlands News Association for many years.

'Last of the Boy Soldiers' is his first published novel and it draws on his own experiences of National Service. Since those days, as one of the last to be called up to serve their two-year conscription, John has become a highly respected advisor to a number of athletes on all matters of health and fitness. He still maintains a rigorous fitness regime, preferring to spend time in the gym to watching television or drifting subconsciously into retirement. Married, with two children and four grandchildren, John still lives in the West Midlands where he acts as chief reviewer for the Internet publishing company, 'Books 4 Publishing.com' on a part time basis that allows him time to continue with his writing.

To all those who signed on and survived their two year punishment; those who learned that comradeship would see them through and that the friendships they forged would never be equalled, and to those in authority who made life hell but made men strong.

I salute you all.

I am delighted to write a foreword for 'Last of The Boy Soldiers'. John Oliver tells a story about National Service, which will amuse those who did it and entertain those who didn't. The humour is just as it was, down to earth and realistic. It also portrays the agonies and frustrations of basic training – reminding me of my own two years conscription in the R.A.O.C.

I would like to wish him every success with the book and look forward to reading the follow-up.

Sir Henry Cooper OBE, KSG

Chapter 1

Between the ages of 18 and 21, all young men who could name three European countries, allow their testicles to be fondled without either returning the compliment or punching the doctor, and correctly assemble a four piece jigsaw, could expect a buff-coloured envelope stamped with the letters OHMS.

Mine arrived at 7:28 a.m. on a damp, dismal morning, delivered by an overweight postman wearing a uniform made for someone smaller. His smile suggested he knew something I didn't. "Is this what you've been waiting for?" he said. His reluctance to release the letter produced further clues. "Looks like you'll soon be in uniform."

"So long as it fits better than yours." I snatched the letter, unable to think of a more suitable insult, slamming the door in his face, anxious to discover the army's plans without interruption. We all knew what to expect having watched friends and workmates disappear as innocent young men, returning two years later as men of the world, extolling well-rehearsed stories of travel, adventure and the occasional visit to the MO.

Only the choice of regiment and posting held any real mystery. Far East, Middle East, Gibraltar, Germany. Logically I should be joining the R.E.M.E. or Royal Engineers but I would soon discover logic wasn't part of army policy.

With an air of resignation, I tore open the envelope, no longer dreaming of exotic locations, just hoping it would be within a fifty-mile radius of Wolverhampton, my home town. I read it through with a growing apprehension reminding me of a young lad about to lose his virginity. You wait years for it to happen, planning, fantasising, and then, when the opportunity arrives, you're still not ready.

A similar feeling preceded the much debated medical examination, where stony-faced doctors looked at, listened to, and felt an assortment of anxious males growing even more personally concerned at the realisation we were clearly not all born equal.

This stark foretaste of joining an organisation where modesty is frowned upon and imperfections ridiculed prompted many a quivering wreck to complain of burst eardrums and fallen arches. The more desperate confessed to child molesting or a preference for wearing women's clothes, while bed-wetters were reassured with the knowledge that most new recruits did it during training.

The vast majority of lads went at 18, reducing the risk of having to leave a young wife either pregnant or rampant – neither of which were acceptable grounds for avoiding National Service.

An apprenticeship in machine shop engineering delayed my call-up for three years, during which time talk of ending conscription became a real prospect. We were no longer engaged in warfare - just the occasional skirmish by tin pot dictators overloaded with medals and a desire to rule the world. These spasmodic outbreaks could be easily contained by the regular army supported by upstanding territorials, available most weekends throughout the summer.

As each day passed, it soon became clear there would be no last minute reprieve. Barring accident or illness, I was destined to become Gunner Tramp of the Royal Artillery.

Living at home allowed the kind of freedom married lads of my age soon began to envy. I never had to explain my whereabouts, hand over a wage packet, or apologise for something I hadn't done. Neither did I have a 25-year mortgage around my neck or the worry of struggling to keep up hire purchase payments on goods I couldn't really afford. Not that I hadn't considered flat sharing. All night parties and loose women featured high on my list of priorities. Until Dad died, and then I had Ma to consider.

I was about seventeen at the time, two years into an uninspiring apprenticeship thanks to an instructor whose flat Black Country accent forced many a young lad to reconsider his career. Then again, Mr Fisher, the only white coat in a sea of dark blue overalls, never did get excited which no doubt accounted for his wife's infidelity with anyone who was remotely interesting.

Even the arrival of a grim-faced policeman, complete with bicycle clips and gloves, failed to divert my attention from the scantily clad young ladies posing seductively amongst the pages of Spick and Span – many a young lad's introduction to the mysteries of women's underwear.

A nervous cough announced the instructor's silent arrival before I could slide the well-thumbed magazine across the desk towards Barry Brookes, a bespectacled train spotter more interested in the figures 4-4-4 than 36-24-36.

"It's his." I replied nodding in Barry's direction. "I keep telling him he'll go blind."

"No it isn't," he exploded, face turning crimson as a chorus of *Yes it is!* echoed around the room. The instructor wasn't interested, although he did allow himself a cursory glance at the offending item before lightly touching my shoulder. "Joe, I wonder if you would mind stepping into the corridor. Constable Riley wants a word with you."

"I bet he's been flashing his todger around," sneered Sid Price, whose obsession with exposing his own todger had already earned him two cautions and a bloody nose. "Either that or he's put some tart up the stick."

"Probably Fisher's wife," whispered Sid's mate, rubbing his testicles to emphasise the point - something no-one else had ever wanted to do, apart from a scoutmaster who insisted on sharing a sleeping bag during a three day jamboree alongside the River Severn.

The instructor's glare silenced further comments as twenty pairs of eyes followed my exit from the room, eager to discover the reason for this sudden interruption.

"Joe, I'm afraid I have bad news for you." PC 354 removed his cap, placing the gloves inside before gently ushering me away from prying eyes. "It's your father."

I waited as he struggled to find the words, his short, stumpy fingers sliding slowly through the greying hair. "He's had an accident."

His face ruled out the possibility of a sprained ankle and the recurrence of an old back problem hardly warranted police involvement.

"What sort of an accident?"

Constable Riley hated three things - arresting drunks, working with policewomen, and conveying bad news, unlike many of his colleagues who revelled in all three. "Serious, I'm afraid."

Somewhere in the distance a door opened and closed sending a gust of wind swirling along the deserted corridor. The disturbance prompted him into action, confirming my worst fears in a rush of words.

"There's no easy way to say this, Joe. Your father's dead!" PC Riley paused long enough to wipe away the first beads of sweat gathering on his furrowed brow. "He was working at the pit face when it happened."

I waited for further details but either he didn't know, or he wouldn't say.

"Has Ma been told?" My question clearly surprised him, or perhaps it was my lack of emotion as I tried to make sense of it all.

"Er … yes. WPC Walters is with her now. She's very good at these sorts of things." He replaced the cap, gently easing the strap over the beginnings of a double chin. "Is there anyone I can contact to collect you? Neighbour? Relative?"

"No thanks, I've got my bike."

I left him standing in the corridor, a forlorn figure looking nearer to tears than I did. Having delivered the bad news he pulled on the bike clips and gloves, hoping the Raleigh Roadster was still in one piece. His last visit to Collins Engineering resulted in two flat tyres and a missing bell, the replacement of which didn't have quite the same impact in an emergency.

No one spoke when I returned to the lecture room to collect my things. If they did, I wasn't listening. I acknowledged Mr Fisher's concern with a brief nod – giving the impression I understood, when I didn't. The sun warmed my back on the way home then, perhaps as a mark of respect it disappeared behind a black cloud. I reached the front door in a state of confusion, legs trembling and heart pounding, unsure of how I would cope with Ma's reaction.

Inside, the drawn curtains changed everything to colourless shapes and yet it was the silence that finally overwhelmed me. As so often in the past, she was there to comfort me, brushing away the tears with soft, soothing sounds. Suddenly I was a child again.

Women of Ma's age were not given to emotional outbursts. Having lived through two World Wars they were expected to maintain a stiff upper lip and just get on with it.

The last time we were so close, she tried explaining why Grandad had been taken from us. For three years I thought he was in heaven, surrounded by angels. Then I discovered he was actually in prison surrounded by netting, serving eight years for misappropriating union funds.

We both found the funeral something of an ordeal, prolonged by the Yorkshire vicar's sermon explaining why Dad wasn't really dead, just resting till the day we would all meet up again. His theory appeared much less convincing the following day when he presented us with the bill and a box of ashes.

Ma did her best after Dad died, skimping and saving in order for me to complete my apprenticeship. I wanted to find more lucrative employment, a job that would ease the financial pressures, but she dismissed the idea insisting it was Dad's wish that I should qualify as an engineer. "There'll always be a need for skilled craftsmen," he had said, emphasising the word skilled, "so don't end up like me, digging coal for a living."

In those days the men had very little choice. Either they were down the mines from dawn to dusk or in the army fighting for King and country in a foreign land for a cause they never really understood.

At least I managed to continue piano lessons, unknown to anyone but Ma and Miss Drew, a highly respected music teacher who actually saw potential in my weekly visits and gave me unwavering encouragement

I was able to use the well-polished Steinway to express feelings I could neither say nor describe. A far cry from the coarseness of factory life, where any spark of artistic ability was constantly ridiculed.

Although I disliked the boredom and discipline for learning piano scales, it had its reward when I eventually mastered Debussy's *Clare De Lune*. Later additions to my repertoire included Sinding's *Rustle of Spring* and the haunting *Hebrides Overture* by Mendelssohn. Further musical glory ended when Miss Drew suffered a series of strokes, each one paralysing a different part of her body until she could do little more than move her head and feet.

Her successor, a thin hatchet-faced spinster with a great beak of a nose on which hung a pince-nez, had neither the time nor patience to maintain my interest against the growing attraction of the opposite sex.

Although the piano lessons had to go, I never lost my love for classical music, thanks to the efforts of Miss Drew, who sadly passed away just a few short weeks before my call-up papers arrived.

Ma cleared the breakfast things in her usual brisk manner, disappearing into the kitchen amidst a series of plate scraping and saucepan rattling sounds, sounds suggesting some kind of stew for later.

The customary cup of tea arrived but this time without the smile as she considered my imminent departure. "Where did you say it was again?" she asked.

"The Royal Artillery camp in Gravesend, Kent. It's on the River Thames, opposite Tilbury Docks … just south east of London."

She was unimpressed with my geographical knowledge, merely leaning forward to adjust the tablecloth so that I could see how thin the greying hair lay over her head. "At least you're not going abroad."

"I'm only there for basic training then I could be posted anywhere in the world. Gibraltar. Hong Kong. Germany."

"Germany!" She made it sound obscene. "Oh, I don't want you going there, it isn't safe."

"Ma, the war's been over 15 years. I don't think they want to start another one."

She clearly didn't share my confidence, wringing her hands as the prospect of World War Three loomed ever closer. "That's what they said in 1918, the war to end all wars. Twenty years later they were at it again."

No point trying to argue the situation - Ma's generation would never trust the old enemy so I finished my tea and prepared for work. "See you later."

"Don't forget your sandwiches."

I accepted them with a brief nod, pausing in front of the hall mirror to remove a persistent black head. "Cheese again?"

"Well I know you like it."

I also liked liver and onions but not every bloody day. I shoved them into my duffle coat pocket, wishing she would be a little more inventive with her culinary skills. Workmate, Bernie, a highly respected pigeon breeder, constantly at war with the neighbours, had different sandwiches every day of the week. If he worked Saturday it messed up the sequence and he had to sleep with the pigeons.

I stepped into a world of half-empty cars and overcrowded buses edging their way past grim looking pedestrians, coughing and spitting as they inhaled their first cigarette of the day. There certainly wasn't much to smile about at 7:30 on a cold, damp morning - faced with the prospect of working nine hours in semi-darkness, listening to a sixty year-old lathe operator explaining the technicalities of the female orgasm.

During the second break of the morning, with machines temporarily silenced, the lads took advantage of a well-earned rest, debating world issues and how they should be solved. While I read the news in common with everyone else, I had no intention of concerning myself with Fidel Castro's strong-arm tactics, instead using the time to notify management of my impending departure to pastures new.

Bill Parker, ex-apprentice who mysteriously rose to the position of departmental manager, rarely ventured from the safety of his office, having lost all credibility amongst shop floor workers while attempting to reduce the number of tea breaks and dictating who should work overtime. At the strike meeting shop stewards called him a 'control freak' insisting we made a stand before he tried to impose even more restrictions. Fortunately, the board of directors understood our concerns, insisting he made a public apology over the newly-installed Tannoy system.

I went in to his office.

"What do you want, Tramp?" William Parker, more commonly known as nosey, had no intention of returning my smile. "I'm busy."

I hesitated, his newspaper was open at the racing page. "I can always come back when you've finished picking the winners."

He didn't appreciate the comment, angrily sweeping the newspaper from his desk along with a leather-bound appointment book - unopened since January, two betting slips and a red bakelite telephone that shattered on impact with the concrete floor. "You stupid bastard!" Parker shouted. "Now look what you've made me do."

He expected me to retrieve the items but I remained upright, awaiting his next outburst. It didn't take long. "How the bloody hell can I do anything now the phone's broken?"

"Isn't there another one you can use to ring your bets through?"

With his back pressed hard against the black swivel chair, he considered the consequence of an instant dismissal - recalling a similar incident which ultimately led to a three day strike and another humiliating climb down. "Why don't you just piss off out of my sight!"

"I thought you'd like to hear my good news, Mr Parker."

"Unless you've got an incurable disease or another job, I'm not interested."

"My call-up papers have arrived. I'll be leaving next week. Still if you're not interested."

Having been disliked since leaving school, and more than likely while he was at school, William Parker had no intention of trying to rectify the situation. "Saves me giving you the bloody sack."

"You can't sack me, I haven't done anything."

"And don't think I haven't noticed." He lit the fifth cigarette of the day, inhaling smoke into his already congested lungs. "You're last to arrive in a morning and first to leave at night. Beats me why you bother coming in at all."

"I enjoy the company."

"Bollocks. We can't have people turning up for work whenever they feel like it."

"Why not? Your secretary does. You're always giving her days off."

"That's not true ... well not exactly." Mentioning Beryl always reddened his features, a condition Mrs Parker worried about. "Occasionally I give her one."

"I know, we often watch you sneaking in to the stores together."

For the first time in his life, the manager did three things at once. He stood upright, kicked the chair backwards, and thumped the desk with a white-knuckled fist. "You fucking bastard!" he screamed. "You've done it now!"

Before I could discover exactly what I'd done, the door burst open and in walked Beryl – clearly in a better mood than her boss. "Is that right you've had your call-up papers, Joe?" She squeezed her ample backside between chair and desk, unaware of the tension as she half disappeared behind a cumbersome typewriter. "Harry's just been telling me."

"Yeah, in a few days time I shall be a professional soldier ... might even sign on for twenty one years."

"We'll keep our fingers crossed then," said Bill Parker, ignoring Beryl's raised eyebrows, usually the sign for another trip to the stores. "In the meantime get your arse back to work. That's what we pay you for."

I gave a wry smile before leaving the office, not anticipating a farewell gift from Mr Parker.

After the initial shock of being called-up, I actually started looking forward to the experience. An opportunity to escape the boredom of factory life whilst embarking on a career of travel and adventure. I even considered the possibility of promotion – Captain Tramp had a certain ring of authority, similar to a doctor or man of the cloth.

Not everyone approved of my growing enthusiasm to sample army life. Apart from Ma I had to console Christine West, a 19 year-old part time barmaid with ambitions to rule the catwalk and complete an elocution course.

Next came Susannah, a Woolworth's shop assistant who objected to anyone shortening her name. Her old-fashioned appearance and values left her determined to walk up the aisle a virgin, and nothing I could do or say would change her mind – although vodka almost did the trick.

Another Black Country lass dreaming of stardom inherited her mother's good looks and her father's tendency towards exaggeration. Judy Biggleswade told everyone her dad was a brain surgeon who drove a Bentley Continental and owned a villa in the South of France. In fact he was a postman who had a BSA bike and a caravan in Wales.

We said our last goodbyes with scenes worthy of Romeo and Juliet, swearing undying love combined with promises none of us would ever keep. In a final act of passion I gave Christine and Judy something to remember me by. I just hoped they wouldn't return the compliment nine months later.

On my last night of freedom, friends, workmates and a few complete strangers expecting to see a darts match, gathered at the Royal Oak pub for a farewell drink, the majority determined to give me a proper send-off, while others anticipated free food and drink. This touching gesture lost a little of its meaning when I had to settle the bill.

During a buffet of cheese sandwiches, pork pies and pickled onions, Terry Taylor, an old school friend, who managed to avoid national service by attending the medical examination wearing a Norman Hart-nell creation complete with matching accessories, bored everyone to death reminiscing about our misspent youth before presenting me with a silver plated cigarette lighter inscribed *J Tramp*. I thanked all those involved, promising to begin smoking right away.

The first words of advice came from Arthur Rawlings, militant shop steward who began life sweeping floors. His uncompromising attitude and colourful language earned him an office, a secretary, and authority to halt production at the slightest hint of interference from management. Arthur's inability to read and write didn't prevent him lecturing me on the numerous advantages of living under a communist regime. Quite an achievement considering he'd never travelled further than Blackpool for the Labour Party conference.

I soon tired of his admiration for Marx, finally shoving a cigar in his mouth and shouting, "Now show us the funny walk, Groucho."

He responded in the usual way, calling for a sit-down strike until I apologised. Outvoted fifty to one, he called me an imperialist puppet, promising to inform the Kremlin of my conduct to ensure I never achieved Russian citizenship.

As the evening progressed, with voices becoming louder and less clear, I was asked to have words with Charlie Turner, a bull of a man with uncontrollable hair and a temper to match. Charlie, a welder by trade, wore his usual T-shirt complete with burns and offensive sweat stains. He was banned from most of the pubs in Wolverhampton, a list that would soon include this one if the barman had his way.

"I'm only carrying out orders, sir. If you want another drink you'll have to ask the gaffer." The nervous looking barman continued drying glasses, moving further away from the bar as Charlie moved closer.

"Pour me another drink, you little turd, or I'll put this between your fucking eyes!"

Tony the barman looked around for help as a huge fist shook before his eyes. In his dreams he could handle any situation - unfortunately, he was now wide awake. "It's more than my job's worth, sir."

"Hello, Charlie. Everything alright?" I said as I approached the bar.

Charlie gave me a long bleary-eyed glare before deciding I was interfering. "Piss off and mind your own business."

"C'mon, Charlie … it is my party after all." I included a friendly smile, reluctant to close the gap between us. "You wouldn't want to spoil it for me."

Charlie wasn't listening, swaying backwards and forwards on the balls of his feet like an overweight boxer unsure where the next blow was coming from. His eyes settled once more on the unfortunate barman. "Now are you going to pour me that fucking drink, or shall I do it myself?"

Tony shook his head and continued drying the same glass, wishing his enrolment in unarmed combat classes had run its full course. "I'm sorry, sir, customers are not allowed behind the bar."

"We'll soon see about that."

I stood in the way, hoping to avoid further trouble, aware that the barman was slowly retreating. "Leave it out, Charlie. You know what the gaffer's like. He's probably ringing the police right now."

Even as the words came out I knew it was a waste of time. You couldn't reason with blokes like Charlie Turner even when they were sober.

With one brawny arm, accompanied by a suggestion as to what I should do with my reproductive organs, he swept me aside but the panelled wall held me upright and I still beat him to the end of the bar. "You ain't going round there, Charlie."

He lunged forward, making my blow to the stomach appear far more effective as it buried itself deep into the soft, rubbery flesh, turning Charlie's look of anger into one of surprise. I finished the demolition with a vicious knee into a delicate part of his anatomy, standing back in case he harboured thoughts of retaliation – but he simply sank to the floor, both hands clutching his throbbing testicles. "You fucking bastard! I'll fucking get you for this."

I stepped closer, fists tightly clenched, recognising the danger in letting him rise. But he stayed down, convinced his nightly jaunts to the red light district were a thing of the past.

The barman glanced anxiously towards a door marked 'private' arming himself with a second tea towel. "The gaffer should be here any second. He's only upstairs."

Having temporarily solved the problem, I had no intention of hanging around for a possible replay, and headed quickly towards the lounge and, hopefully, a more relaxed atmosphere.

With the earlier fracas forgotten, I began to enjoy myself, even smiling at jokes that weren't funny the first time around.

"Charlie's looking for you, Joe. Doesn't seem very happy."

Before the speaker could be located, the brawny welder came into view, one hand entwined in his groin, the other carrying something shiny and cumbersome. Having sorted him out once I knew I was quite capable of doing it again - until a metal bar stool headed towards me at 30 mph. My final recollection centred on the patterned Axminster carpet as it approached at a similar speed to the stool.

Chapter 2

My eyes opened slowly, and closed quickly as the early morning sun streamed through clumsily-drawn bedroom curtains. I tried again using just one eye but the brightness remained so I gave up, rolling awkwardly onto my stomach, both arms pushed beneath an old feather pillow showing all the signs of a restless sleep.

A muffled explosion raised my head, growing closer and closer until I could locate the cause. With my nose screwed up tight I wafted the blankets three times in succession – making a mental note to remove pickled onions from my diet.

Gradually the previous night's events began to unfold - Terry Taylor's uninspiring speech, the presentation, and my confrontation with Charlie Turner. Even the endless words of advice came flooding back, most of them endorsing the advantages of casual sex. After that - nothing. Just questions: How did I arrive home? Who undressed me? And where the hell did that egg-sized lump come from?

My hand again swept through the uncombed crew-cut but it was still there, distorting the shape of my head. Following a process of elimination, I decided Banks's bitter was probably to blame. Wouldn't be the first time ten pints had affected my legs. I checked once more before dismissing it. There were far more important things to worry about.

With reluctant anticipation, I hauled myself from the comfortable warm bed, dressing in slow motion as I looked around the room where my journey had begun twenty one years ago.

There were bird's eggs in trays - those still intact no longer recognisable from their colour - watched over by a stuffed kestrel, staring out from behind the broken glass of a display case. A collection of model cars filled an old shoe box, displaying the date, size and 1957 asking price for a pair of men's slip-ons.

Pride of place went to my records, mostly 78's, stacked in three neat piles along a pine shelf erected six years ago as a temporary measure. Duke Ellington, Nelson Riddle and Artie Shaw providing the background, while Sinatra, Como etc., produced sounds most of us could only dream about. I blew the dust off Swan Lake, and ran my fingers over Handel's Water Music, wondering if I would ever see them again – but the moment passed.

With a shrug of resignation, I headed downstairs dragging a large leather suitcase full of items I would probably never use again, including a Diana 4.5 mm air pistol buried beneath layers of clothes. Why, I can't imagine: the army never mentioned anything about bringing your own gun.

I even contemplated removing the stickers decorating the suitcase but it would take far too long and they did look rather impressive. Majorca, Benidorm, Paris, Malta, Rhyl. On second thoughts I scratched out Rhyl.

I ate breakfast in silence, aware that it could be my last decent meal for two years. I debated whether army food deserved its poor reputation, decided it probably did and promptly shoved in another packet of biscuits.

Eventually I was ready to leave, dreading the final goodbye which was never going to be easy. I could hardly walk past the kitchen shouting, 'I'm off now, Ma, see you in a couple of years.'

She was in her usual place, standing quietly at the sink, hands immersed in soapy water preparing herself for my inevitable departure. "Have you got everything, love?"

"Er … yes. I think so."

We stood in silence, both staring straight ahead, unsure of what to do or say. I remembered the countless times she asked for a tap washer to be fitted or a proper clothes line erected, instead of having to use two trees, one of them in next door's garden. 'I'll get someone in,' she would say. 'You haven't the time.'

She always did make excuses for me, taking the pressures when I should've been a little more considerate, but that's what mothers did. Now it was too late. I could hardly make up for twenty one years of neglect in two minutes.

"Ma, I have to go now or I shall miss the train. You wouldn't want me arriving late on my first day."

I tried to keep things light-hearted the way I did with everything but she always knew if I was hurt or worried. "I don't know what I shall do without you, love."

I reached for her hand, surprised by its warmth. Then again it had come straight from the washing bowl. "It's alright, Ma, it'll soon be over."

She wasn't quite sure what I meant, but nodded anyway, unable to hide the tremor in her voice. "I know, love. I know."

As she turned to face me I could see the anguish etched into her face alongside the wrinkles that shouldn't be there on a woman in her forties. Funny how you can live with someone all your life and yet never really look at them. Now I could see it all. The struggle to carry on after Dad died, doing without in order for me to attend college and complete an apprenticeship. The hardship of surviving the war years – which in her case didn't improve much in peacetime. Nowadays the majority of widows would remarry or live it up on the insurance money. But not Ma - her life ended with the death of my father.

I bent low, kissing her cheek, aware of the tears beginning to fall. "I shall have to go, Ma."

Unable to speak, she answered with a nod, hands still holding mine. I wanted to say something loving but words failed me, or perhaps the occasion proved too much – so I made do with a squeeze, mumbling a choked goodbye before rushing out into the cool, fresh air.

I could hear the soft gentle sobs as I walked out of her life, fighting back the tears threatening to send me running back to her arms. I couldn't even turn around, so I carried on, trying to remember when I stopped the goodnight kiss or affectionate hug. That was the problem with becoming a man – you forgot about being a son.

I decided against using the bus, hoping the light breeze would clear away the tears in case I met anyone I knew. I could hardly put it down to hay fever in the middle of October.

An ambulance raced by startling all but the stone deaf as it broke every rule in the highway code in an attempt to save some poor sod who probably didn't want to live anyway.

Ten minutes later I strode through the heavy glass doors of Wolver-hampton railway station and approached the booking office clerk who was busily engaged on a full-scale refurbishment of her nails. She looked up, decided I was unimportant and continued filing. I placed the travel pass in front of her, frowning as she carefully applied the nail varnish. "Do you want me to wait until you've finished?" I asked sarcastically.

She eyed the pass with suspicion, decided it wasn't a forgery and exchanged it for a ticket which I carefully scrutinised before stepping aside for the next customer.

"She'll be with you in about ten minutes, mate. Just her toenails to do."

After purchasing a newspaper and chocolate I headed for the platforms, ticket in one hand, suitcase in the other.

"You going to join up then, cock?" enquired the ticket collector looking in two directions at once.

I tried not to stare as he checked the details. Unable to decide which was the good eye, I said, "Is it that obvious?"

"It is to me." Both his elbows rested on the barrier and I knew it would be a long conversation. "They all pass this way you know. Army, navy, air force. You soon get to know who's going where. Now I put you down as a navy man."

"No. Army."

"Royal Engineers?"

"No. Artillery."

He scratched the end of his chin with dirt-stained fingernails, surprised things weren't going his way. "In that case you'll be going to Woolwich Arsenal, home of the gunners."

Whether he was referring to soldiers or footballers I had no idea, nor did I want to find out. "Well, I must be off…"

"I did my national service in the signals. Now, when was it?"

"During the war?"

"I'm not that bloody old, you cheeky sod." He scratched his chin once more, one eye staring into space, the other just … staring. "How old do you think I am?" He mistook my lack of interest for politeness. "Go on, you won't insult me."

I immediately proved him wrong. "Sixty?"

"Are you taking the piss? I'm not even fifty."

Having ruined his day I had every-intention of leaving, until he grabbed my arm. "I may be a bit older than you, but I can still look after myself. From what I can see, today's army is full of queers. None of those in my day. God help us if we're ever invaded."

"They'll probably have to bring you lot back to sort it out." I gave him a brief inspection, removing his hand from my sleeve. "You still look in pretty good shape."

He pulled in his stomach, the effect swelling his chest. "I try to look after myself. Plenty of long walks, gardening, things like that." A twinge of arthritis reminded him of the problem but in common with high blood pressure and a weak bladder he chose to ignore it. "Do you know I reckon I could still get through basic training, nine mile runs, rope climbing, unarmed combat." He glanced down, unable to hold the fat in any longer. "Might have to lose a few pounds, but it's all there."

"Yes, I can see that."

"At one time I could place both hands flat on the floor. I wonder...."

He disappeared from view. Once. Twice. When he didn't come back up, I peered over the barrier. "Who are you hiding from?"

"I'm not bloody hiding, my back's gone." A hand floundered about as he tried unsuccessfully to rise. "I need someone to straighten me out."

"Do you want me to ring a psychiatrist?"

"Piss off, you little bastard!"

"I've never heard anything like it," gasped an elderly lady standing nearby. "British Rail used to be so helpful ... and polite."

"I know ... all I asked for was a ticket."

She pushed me aside leaning angrily over the barrier. "Now look here, young man. You may be a cripple but that's no excuse for rudeness."

I didn't wait for the response, assuming it would be far from apologetic. I made my way across the graffiti-covered footbridge to platform three, joining a handful of businessmen waiting for the 7:55 train to Euston.

Their solemn faces suggested this was a trip they did regularly, maybe every day. It would have to be a bloody good job for me to travel that distance. I could never get to work on time when it was just up the road.

The train arrived ten minutes late, discharging a mixture of smoke and water as it shunted backwards and forwards before coming to a screeching halt. Within seconds, the waiting figures were aboard, disappearing into various compartments, either to do battle with a crossword or study the latest share prices. Others closed their eyes pretending to catnap, a way of letting fellow passengers know they didn't want to be disturbed.

I found it difficult to relax, fidgeting in the seat until the rhythmical sounds coming from the track began to have a calming effect, much to the relief of my travelling companions who assumed I had some form of nervous disorder.

We eventually arrived at Euston station fifteen minutes late, resulting in a mad rush for buses, taxis or the tube. I chose the latter, saving time and money on my way to Charing Cross and the 12:40 for Gravesend. That final leg of the journey involved six unscheduled stops, leaving me tired, late and hungry by the time I reached my destination.

I half expected to be greeted by the Royal Artillery band, followed by a personal welcome from the commanding officer, but the station remained deserted, apart from a porter with a lisp whose dreams of emulating Ronnie Ronalde disappeared when two of his teeth were knocked out.

Ten minutes of watching and waiting produced nothing more than aching legs and a rumbling stomach, leaving me debating the choice between finding my own way to camp or catching the next train home.

Before I could decide, a grim looking soldier approached, arms swinging almost horizontally as he quickly closed the distance between us. "You're late!" he barked, exaggerating the halt. "The train arrived twelve minutes ago."

I waited for him to relax, or smile even, but his face and stance demanded an explanation.

"Er... I didn't know what to do."

"You didn't know what to do?" His voice went up and down the scale. "No good to the army if you don't know what to do." Any thoughts of defining my statement evaporated as his face came closer, forcing mine back in order to avoid contact. "This is a man's world, boy, not fucking playschool!"

I enjoyed the comparison.

Unfortunately, he didn't. "Are you smirking, boy?"

For a moment I thought he may lash out but the incident passed, although I could tell it wouldn't take much to push him over the edge.

"Do you know what these are?" He pointed to each stripe in turn, slowly, deliberately. "They signify I'm a bombardier, therefore you will address me as Bombardier Hawkins. Not mate, mucker or me old cock sparrow. Is that clear?"

"Yes, Bombardier Hawkins."

"I can't hear you."

"Yes, Bombardier Hawkins."

"I still can't HEAR YOU, BOY!"

"Yes, Bombardier Hawkins!" I yelled, unable to believe I was being bullied into a shouting match. "Perfectly clear, Bombardier Hawkins."

He moved his 5' 7" body back two paces, almost challenging me to comment on his lack of height. At 6' 1" I towered over him but that proved to be my only advantage.

"Now smarten up, shoulders back, chest out. Move it! Move it!"

I wasn't quite sure which way to move, a dilemma that didn't go unnoticed.

"Are you going to stand there all day, boy?"

"But I thought …"

"Don't think, the army pays me to think. You just do as you're told." His arm indicated the general direction. "Now get outside."

I obeyed the instruction, aware of the interest as passers-by witnessed my first public humiliation, followed by another as I hesitated at the footpath.

"Frightened of the traffic, boy?"

"No, bombardier, I was just …"

"Shut it. This isn't a fucking sightseeing trip. Now get your arse into the back of that lorry."

A Bedford three-tonner sat opposite, glistening under numerous coats of paint diligently applied by intelligent young men using tooth-brushes. I waited as a black Standard Vanguard crawled past, the elderly driver acknowledging our presence with a toothy grin. Regrettably only one of us returned the greeting.

"Wipe that smirk oft your face, Tramp, or I'll have you locked up for soliciting."

I hurried across the road as the engine roared into life, a vibrating exhaust pipe squeezing out clouds of smelly, blue smoke. The hatless driver stared vacantly into space, fingers drumming on the metal steering wheel. He had one stripe, tattoos on his knuckles, and the kind of face that gave children nightmares.

As I approached, he leaned out of the cab window and spat on the pavement - his way of telling me to stop. "Name?"

"Tramp. And you are?" I stretched up on my toes studying the letters across his bony knuckles. "Rose?"

He already had one foot on the ground as Bombardier Hawkins stepped between us, hand firmly positioned against the driver's chest. "That's enough. We can't have soldiers brawling in the street. Leave that to the civilians."

The lanky driver thought otherwise. "Do you know what that bastard called me?"

"Not now, Charlie."

"We can't let him get away with that."

Bombardier Hawkins could, at least for the moment. "Charlie, there's a time and place for everything, and this is neither the time nor the place." His attention reverted to me. "You're not getting off to a very good start, are you, boy? Now get in the back of that fucking lorry."

I threw my case over the tailboard, and clambered in watched by two pairs of eyes outside and one pair inside.

After settling back on the hard wooden bench I turned to speak, but the nervous face looked away so I gave up the idea, preferring to contemplate my initial assessment of army life. Perhaps it was all play acting, a way of introducing us to discipline. Perhaps beneath the shouting and bullying, both NCOs were really nice blokes. I considered the possibility, but only briefly before deciding they were both control freaks with a limited grasp of the English language, hiding behind a uniform, intent on making our lives a misery.

Ten minutes and seven potholes further on, the driver slammed his size twelve boot on the brake pedal, throwing us both to the floor in a tangle of flailing arms and legs.

"Sorry," blurted my travelling companion from somewhere in the vicinity of my backside. "I couldn't help it."

The voice continued apologising until I spoke up. "Don't worry about it, mate. Wasn't your fault."

We were still struggling to unravel ourselves when the lance bombardier's head appeared over the tailboard. "What's going on here then? A fucking sex orgy?" He adjusted his beret, now shrunk to half its original size. "We don't allow that sort of thing in the army. You should've joined the air force."

I remained silent, unlike Melvyn Jones, brought up believing an apology was preferable to confrontation. "Sorry, bombardier. My fault. I can assure you it won't happen again."

Dodds, using every inch of his six foot four frame, towered over the cowering figure, rapidly reducing to four foot two. "You're a pathetic little shit, Jones. What are you?"

"A pathetic little shit, bombardier."

"I can't hear you, Jones."

"A pathetic little shit, bombardier."

"And what about the rest of your family?"

"They're all pathetic little shits, bombardier."

With Hawkins having disappeared, I no longer felt so intimidated. "Why don't you leave him alone?"

I stood my ground as the gangling NCO came over, jabbing a tattooed finger into my chest. I knew it wasn't going to be a lesson in eloquence.

He confirmed my suspicion. "You bastard. I'm going to be battering you tomorrow. Might even start to-*fucking*-day!"

Chapter 3

We stood quietly beside the guardroom - a dozen fresh-faced young men trying to make sense of it all. A few drifted together swapping first impressions with words of bravado, much to the amusement of the soldier on guard, an immaculately turned out gunner recalling the time when he said similar things. Others stood alone, still clutching cases and carrier bags, unsure what to do or where to go. These were the ones who would cry into their pillows at night, never quite coming to terms with life in the military.

Looking around, I could see all shapes and sizes. Lads well over six feet, their beanpole bodies bent at the knees and shoulders in an attempt to remain inconspicuous. Billy Bunter look-alikes who blamed everyone else for their chubby appearances, and short arses with their built-up shoes and inferiority complex. Even the faces differed, making it hard to believe they were all between 18 and 21 years old.

Immediately to our right was the hallowed parade ground with its perimeter marked by looping sections of thick, white rope supported on similarly coloured posts. A lone seagull landed in the middle, strutted around like a feathered variety of the sergeant-major, and then paused, showing its contempt in the usual way.

"That's one mess they're not getting me to clear up," Tony Lister said, adjusting the collar on his leather jacket, trying to imagine how Elvis Presley would react. "Let the thick regulars do it." With everyone watching, he sauntered over to the edge of the parade ground and placed a crepe-soled shoe on the rope before lighting a cigarette and flicking the used match on to the litter free square.

While one or two were impressed by this show of arrogance, most were of the opinion the outfit looked far more intimidating than he ever could, an impression shared by a Sergeant Jenkins.

His sudden appearance gradually silenced the onlookers who, one by one, turned their attention to the stranded gunner. His moment of glory was about to end.

"Soldier!" The sergeant's voice lacked the volume of Dodds or

Hawkins but there was no mistaking the look of anger on his face. "Come here."

To his credit, Tony Lister wasn't about to be hurried, finding time to enjoy another long, leisurely drag on the cigarette, reducing its length by at least an inch before unenthusiastically obeying the command.

Unfortunately for Lister, nobody messed with Sergeant Jenkins - not fellow NCOs, senior officers … or new recruits. There was a long list of people who lived to regret ever meeting Sergeant Jenkins. The list was just about to be extended. "What's your name, gunner?"

The Presley admirer began to relax, even risking another drag on the cigarette. "Tony Lister."

Having fought the Japanese in Malaya and the Germans in North Africa, Jenkins wasn't about to be provoked by someone who'd only ever fired a water pistol. "Where did that black eye come from, gunner?"

"What black eye?"

The sergeant's right fist shot out and back with equal speed. "That one."

Lister hit the floor. The eye started swelling immediately. He wanted to object but the sergeant's expression warned him not to.

"I'll ask you again, gunner. Where did that black eye come from?"

Everyone held their breath as the seconds ticked by. He could either become a hero, calling on the rest of us as witnesses, or say nothing and risk losing all credibility.

"I er... walked into something."

The sergeant nodded approval. "I bet you won't do it again, soldier."

"No, sergeant."

"Are you sure, soldier?"

"Yes, sergeant."

He joined the rest of us, one eye rapidly closing, the other either watery or tearful "Bastard!" he mumbled, staring at the floor. "Bloody bastard!"

Little else was said during the next twenty minutes, until our numbers were increased by even more recruits, equally confused and no doubt regretting their superior physical condition, which at that moment looked a little suspect.

There were a few half-hearted nods plus the usual words of greeting but these soon dried up as inactivity and a feeling of growing despair began to infiltrate our minds.

"We've been here for over an hour doing bugger-all." complained a Welshman whose lilting voice reminded me of Eisteddfods and the coal mining valleys of the Rhondda. He cleared his throat as if to practice the scales. "I'm going to sit down, sod 'em." He straddled a shabby looking case which broadened out under his weight and looked surprised when no-one else responded. "Well come on then .. or are you all frightened?"

The way he emphasised the 't' removed any threat from his voice, encouraging others to speak out.

"I'm not risking it." - "Neither am I. The sergeant might come back." - "The man's a bloody psycho."

Tony Lister pulled up his collar, a move he'd rehearsed a thousand times. "What's the worst he can do?"

"Black your other eye."

"Have you shot?" suggested a bushy haired cockney whose locks would soon be littering the barber's floor. "Worse still, have us all shot."

The Welshman, having failed to get support for his sit down strike, considered his position. "I don't want to get anyone into trouble." After a short pause, he stood up, aware of the sniggers. "I'm only doing it for you lot."

Silence reigned once more, broken only by the occasional bout of wind as people began to feel the effects of empty stomachs.

"One hour, fifteen minutes, that's how long we've been here." The familiar Welsh voice confirmed why he achieved an 'A' in mental arithmetic. "That's seventy five minutes."

From then on he informed us every ten minutes, each one sounding like a countdown to disaster. The next three announcements went unchallenged, but it was only a matter of time.

"One hour, fifty five minutes."

Everyone stared at the speaker, none more so than the Welshman. "No it isn't."

"Oh, yes it is," snapped the newcomer, a severe brushcut emphasising the unusual shape of his ears. "One hour, fifty five minutes, exactly."

The Welshman regained his composure, raising the watch to within four inches of his nose. "It's only one hour, fifty four minutes."

Brushcut wasn't about to back down. "Your watch is slow."

"It bloody well isn't. Yours is fast."

"Bollocks!"

"And bollocks to you."

The argument raged backwards and forwards, the language growing ever more colourful, much to the astonishment of onlookers, shaking their heads in disbelief. Hardly the kind of display you expected from professional soldiers.

"What the fucking hell is going on?" Lance Bombardier Dodds stepped forward, dwarfing both antagonists as they tried to explain.

"It's him, bombardier." The Welshman pointed a threatening finger. "His watch is fast."

"No it isn't." Brushcut realised the need for further evidence. "His is slow and I can prove it." He looked around, a slight smile lightening the stark features. "I checked it with Big Ben."

Dodds addressed the assembled faces. "Okay, which one's Big Ben?" He became suspicious when no one moved, even more so as the smirks began to circulate.

"Big Ben's the clock in the tower of Parliament House, London, bombardier." Brushcut hesitated before continuing the history lesson. "It weighs 132 tons and strikes every fifteen minutes."

Not for the first time, Dodds was reminded of his limited knowledge, calling both men towards him in a voice that spelt trouble. "Give me your watches, you fucking morons."

A reluctance to hand them over turned out to be fully justified when the seething NCO placed both watches on the ground and crushed them with fast rotating movements of his highly polished boots.

Brushcut tried to embark on a rescue mission, whining about the sentimental value, but the bombardier pushed him away.

"Leave it," he barked, "or I'll exchange the watch for your head."

The Welshman's resolve for justice never got off the ground as he remembered the earlier incident with Sergeant Jenkins. "It's only a watch."

Lance Bombardier Dodds didn't like being made to look a fool, vowing to extract revenge sooner rather than later. "Everyone on their feet." The order proved futile with everyone already standing. "Now fall in, move it, move it."

The panic to form a line went from bad to worse as bodies stumbled around, not quite sure where they were supposed to move to.

"I said fall in, not fall down. What a fucking shambles!" The bombardier appeared incapable of talking in a normal voice, assuming we were all hard of hearing as he issued the usual threats of what he would do if we didn't smarten up, and what he would do it with. As a further humiliation we were marched through camp to the accompaniment of loud jeers from small groups of soldiers – most of them having long forgotten their first day.

We eventually shuffled to an untidy halt alongside a large wooden building previously used as a medical centre, guardroom and library. Three years ago it became the quartermaster's store where, if the graffiti was correct, new recruits could be fitted with designer *outfits direct from Paris, see-through uniforms for a night on the* town and *saucy underwear to surprise your buddies.*

More worrying were the crude messages referring to a certain officer's liking for young, fair-haired gunners. At least I was safe unlike the blond lad on my right, determined to let everyone know he wasn't going to be messed about with. "If he tries anything with me I'll soon put this up him."

A shocked gunner who totally misread the comment moved further away. "Dirty buggers!"

"Don't you mean buggerers?" corrected one of his mates.

Inside the actual building were rows of dusty, black dimpled boots, waiting to be brought back to life by eager young hands using vast quantities of spit and polish vigorously applied with the back of a spoon - preferably someone else's spoon.

Other shelves were lined with shirts, sweaters, pyjamas and a variety of underwear guaranteed to turn a girl's head. Even the battledress lacked style while the denims, favoured for everyday wear, appeared to be of a similar material to a potato sack – prompting the expression, 'you look like a bag of shit tied in the middle'.

There were plenty of complaints about the prospect of having to wear unfashionable clothes but none loud enough for the lance bombardier to overhear.

We inched our way along the green-topped counter, less than eager to call out our sizes to a weary-looking regular who clearly hadn't taken a fitness test in years. He was short and round with a yellowish complexion suggesting either too much make up or some form of jaundice. Damp patches discoloured the armpits of his shirt and when he approached you could smell the stale sweat. Cliff Swinton needed a woman's touch, something he hadn't had since a failed relationship drove him into the arms of a sixteen stone docker. He cleared his throat waiting for me to notice him, which I eventually did, ignoring the impatient expression.

"Sixteen and a half collar, tapered to the waist, three buttons on each cuff, preferably in a soft cream or peach."

"Arsehole," he mumbled, dropping three khaki shirts on the counter. I tested the quality showing my disapproval with a turned up nose. "I'm not wearing these ... they'll clash with everyone else's."

A pair of soft, podgy hands prevented me from pushing them away. "Trouser size?"

"Thirty two inch waist, thirty three inside leg, pockets at the front, no turn-ups, belt not braces."

Three pairs landed on top of the shirts - dull brownish twilled cotton, more suited to curtains than clothes. They felt almost like sandpaper and appeared to be bullet-proof.

"I can't put these on, they'll bring me out in a rash."

"See the MO, I only supply the fucking things."

To complete the ensemble, I received a beret the size of a dustbin lid. "What the hell's this?" I enquired, twirling it around on my index finger. "Have they run out of umbrellas?"

Using a hairless forearm, Cliff Swinton wiped the sweat from his brow, hitching up a pair of baggy trousers in a futile attempt to conceal the caseball-size stomach. "Just drop it in water. It'll soon shrink ... everything else does."

I ignored the innuendo and concentrated on carrying everything, which now included an assortment of items the British Museum would probably find interesting. Before I could work out their uses, six of us were separated from the rest and taken to one of the empty barrack huts.

"This is where you're nightmare begins." A lump of phlegm from the mouth of Lance Bombardier Dodds wrapped itself around the door handle. "So put on those aprons, get out those sewing kits and make yourselves at home. Oh, and don't forget the polishing, blancoing, brassing and bedmaking."

He ordered us all inside, grabbing my arm on way past. "Your days are fucking numbered!" he snarled.

I pulled away, stepping gingerly into the hut, avoiding contact with the door handle. "Bloody hell!"

Six iron beds, each supporting a rolled-up mattress, and an equal number of metal lockers were the only items of furniture, apart from a small table previously used for writing suicide notes. There were two windows, neither of which opened, and a solitary light bulb hanging from the roof. Highly polished patterned linoleum covered the floor, deep indentations proving the beds hadn't always been where they now were.

No-one spoke for a long time but you could feel the disappointment as heads shook despairingly and shoulders slumped resignedly.

"Surely they don't expect us to live here."

I recognised the Welsh voice immediately, wondering how many more setbacks there would be. "Perhaps it's all a bad dream." I wished it was, but right now it looked pretty realistic.

My only experience of communal living involved ten days at school camp – somewhere unpronounceable in the heart of Wales selected for its fishing, walking and climbing, none of which could be attempted due to the never-ending rain. The cramped log cabins weren't made for twenty-four hour a day occupation and by day three we were tired of monopoly, sick of doing jigsaws, and fed up with each other's company. Even attempts to poison the cook failed because she preferred eating out. Back at school we were asked to describe the vacation in not more than five hundred words. Those of us who used only two were put on detention for the next six weeks.

"Where's the electric?" A long pause failed to get a response. "I can't see any electric."

"In actual fact you can't see electric." The posh voice decided further explanation was necessary. "You see, electric is invisible."

"Not in our house it isn't. We've got bloody plugs everywhere."

I stared in disbelief as the Lancashire lad searched the room, unable to accept an electricity-free existence. Stan Clark had a ruddy complexion and hair that had seen busier days. At twenty years of age he had been assessed as having a mental age of twelve by an over-familiar army doctor whose idea of an internal examination didn't appeal to Stan. His voice reminded me of George Formby and I wondered if he also played the ukulele.

"Turned out nice again," I said, mimicking the toothy comedian but my attempt to break the ice fell on deaf ears.

"Well that's just great, not one bloody socket." For the third time he studied the light bulb. "There it is."

Only the posh voice bothered to answer. "I'm afraid it's only in the roof. No plugs of any size or description. Anyway at the moment I think we have more important things to concern ourselves with."

The Welshman agreed, but not in the same way. "This place is a dump. We can't live here."

"Why not? It has character."

"It's got bloody woodworm. If we all come to attention at the same time the floor will collapse."

I glanced up, not wishing to extend the pointless banter. "We should be quite safe for some time then."

"I bet those prisoner-of-war films were made here." Stan's earlier concerns over the lack of electric sockets appeared forgotten as he took centre stage. "I can just imagine the escape committee crawling from under the floorboards after a night's digging ... faces red, trousers bulging."

"I think my trousers would be bulging if I'd been under there all night." My comment failed to distract their attention from the more immediate problems.

"Does anyone mind if I commandeer this bed?"

The posh speaking young gunner raised eyebrows again, mainly because no-one expected such manners. This was meant to be every man for himself and yet here we had someone educated and respectful, qualities which could make his two year assignment a traumatic experience.

Outside of the army Steve Clifford's career was assured. An eventual partnership in his father's law firm, membership of the most exclusive clubs in Bristol and the prospect of untold riches – unlike many of us who were destined to start at the bottom and stay there.

Having selected his bed and locker, Steve decided to test the firmness of a soiled mattress, no doubt used by dozens of other bodies for a variety of activities apart from sleeping. "I'll never be able to relax on this. I have an orthopaedic at home, soft to lie on, relieves all tensions and doesn't cost a great deal."

"I've got a girlfriend who does exactly the same," growled a Scotsman, whose scars suggested a tough upbringing. "She doesn't cost a fucking thing."

The contrast between the two men couldn't have been greater and yet here they were thrown together, forced to accept each other's ways and then make the most of it.

"We've now been members of her Majesty's forces...two hours, forty minutes and I still don't like it," announced the Welshman with the air of someone who has reached a crucial decision. "I don't feel I ever will. I think we should complain ... write to somebody important."

"Anyone in particular? The Pope? Queen Elizabeth? Shanghai Lil?"

He ignored my sarcasm and unpacked a canvas holdall. "I remember reading about these blokes who took an officer hostage and then barricaded themselves in until their demands were met."

"And what happened?"

"They raised nearly five hundred quid for charity." Aware of the strange looks, he added, "Well, it was for a good cause."

"We took care of an uncle for years ... thought he was a good cause." The stony-faced Scotsman waited for everyone's attention. "When the old fart died he didn't leave us a fucking penny."

"At least you've got no regrets."

"I bloody well have. We should've killed him sooner."

The prospect of having a murderer in our midst silenced everyone unless they happened to come from Swansea.

"Are we going to complain or not?"

"Don't look at me." My reluctance to get involved obviously required clarification. "I just want to do my two years as painlessly as possible. I don't want any medals or promotion ... someone else can have the stripes."

"I wouldn't mind if the CO wanted to give me one."

"Well if it gets you a stripe, mate."

"I feel the same as him." The only black man in the entire intake nodded in my direction. "I just want to be left alone."

"Greta Garbo said that."

"What for?" I enquired, suddenly aware Stan Clark had chosen the bed next to mine.

"I suppose ... she just wanted to be ... left alone."

We barely had time to catch our breath during the next few hours, working on our kit and living quarters, more out of fear than any sense of pride, but it began to pay off and soon the room took on a lived-in appearance. With so much to do it was impossible trying to carry on any sort of conversation without frequent interruptions.

'How do you do this?' - 'Where does that go?' - 'Who's pinched my polish?' - 'Can I borrow your blanco?' - 'Has anyone got a plaster?'

All linked with expletives ordinary housewives never used. Everything it seems had to be done on the first day – forget the other 729.

Which we did - at about two o'clock in the morning!

Chapter 4

The following day began with a series of bangs, growing progressively louder as the whole bed started to vibrate. I pulled the coarse, prickly blankets higher but the noise continued, almost demolishing the hollow metal bedrail above my head.

"It's half past five," bellowed Lance Bombardier Dodds, bending his lanky frame forward. "You've got ten fucking minutes to get on parade."

When I didn't move, the blankets were unceremoniously whipped away with one hand, while the other used a short staff to prod the only part of my anatomy with any life in it.

"Now get your arse out of bed."

I sat upright and was met by the tattooed fingers as they clamped around my neck. "I don't like the look of you, Tramp."

"I know what you mean. Then again ... it is only five thirty. I improve as the day goes on."

His fingers compressed my Adam's apple, forcing my mouth open in order to breathe, but he still couldn't deflect my unwavering gaze. Releasing his grip, he snarled, "You're a cocky bastard. I'll soon knock that out of you."

For a moment I thought he would start there and then as the staff jabbed against my forehead but the room full of witnesses changed his mind and he stepped back, face tightening with anger. "Nine fucking minutes."

In no time at all I was standing in the foul-smelling latrines alongside an equally bewildered Stan Clark, emptying my bladder with the look of someone not quite sure where he was. I tried not to inhale as another volley of farts rumbled from behind the lavatory door and I wondered if this was a regular occurrence or simply a young sprog who thought he could win the yard-of-ale contest.

"That lance bombardier's certainly got it in for you, Joe. I thought he was going to strangle you at one point." Stan had a final vigorous shake, leaning forward slightly to inspect his assets before tucking them carefully inside regulation coloured pyjamas, legs rolled up in an attempt to avoid unwanted splashes. "He reminds me of Ernest Borgnine in *From Here To Eternity*. Same crazy expression. He couldn't stand Frank Sinatra."

"Well, he's not everyone's cup of tea. Personally I prefer Perry Como."

And so began our basic training, a ritual unchanged for fifty years. Only the faces were different for we were a new generation, not used to words like discipline, respect, bullshit, spit and polish. These expressions were to be fully exploited over the coming months as we dumped lumps of black boot polish mixed with spit onto dimpled toecaps, making them both disappear using a cloth covered index finger.

Leroy excelled at this particular task as he could rotate his finger at breathtaking speed until the dimples were completely obliterated. Steve also managed to convert his into satin smooth objects of envy - unlike Stan who used four tins of polish and always ended up the same colour as Al Jolson.

We were tipped out of bed two hours before sunrise each morning, usually by Lance Bombardier Dodds who took great delight in wrecking the previous night's hard work. With no time to spare, we dashed into the latrines, six shivering recruits jostling for the privilege of washing in cold water and shaving in front of a single mirror, its cracks distorting the anguished faces trying to stem the flow of blood from a dozen cuts. Timex thought he could solve the problem, without using tissue paper, by spraying his face with a plastic coating substance. Unfortunately, it left him with a very shiny appearance, much to the disgust of a duty officer who reported him for wearing make-up on parade.

Every morning before breakfast, the army decreed all equipment, personal or otherwise, should be inspected to ensure blankets were folded to the correct thickness, clothes contained the required number of creases and items included in the locker layout diagram were adjusted to the stipulated angle and distance.

Again Leroy and Steve were rewarded with a curt nod which translated into reluctant admiration, in contrast to the rest of us who had to stand in silence while the inspecting officer relayed the list of faults to an accomplice who recorded them with a despairing shake of the head.

Following frantic reconstruction work for the second time that morning, we were assembled outside for a further inspection carried out by an insignificant second lieutenant, relying on a bushy moustache to improve his air of authority. He avoided eye contact, walking pompously between rows of uninspiring young gunners, each one praying he wouldn't stop to seek their views on army life. It was very difficult to lie when all the squad were listening. At this hour of the morning officers invariably looked more uncomfortable than us, stifling yawns in between reprimanding the usual quota of defaulters. The heinous crimes included feet not exactly in line, beret at the wrong angle, and eyes focusing below the required parallel position; offences that were emphasised with all the solemnity of a prosecutor at the Nuremberg trials. Thankfully, the inspection rarely lasted longer than ten minutes as the lure of the officers' mess overcame any desire to improve the officer's leadership skills.

With breakfast barely digested, we were entrusted to Battery Sergeant Major 'Roddy' Rhodes, an ageing drill instructor far more used to bigger occasions and better turned out squads. He was every inch a soldier, from the sparkling boots which had tramped all over Europe, to the uniform, creased to perfection and worn with pride. He had a sharp and critical eye capable of spotting a dull brass button or a speck of dust at twenty paces. Each blot on your appearance received the customary punishment of ten press-ups, made even more difficult by the weight of his foot resting squarely between your shoulder blades. Anything less than a hundred percent effort left many a young lad with a bloody nose.

"Squad!" His eyes moved suspiciously across the sea of expectant faces, almost challenging someone to make a false move. "Atteeeeenshun!"

After a prolonged clatter of feet, we eventually came to order, much to the despair of BSM Rhodes who was shaking his head at the daunting prospects ahead. He looked round for inspiration, clearly undecided whether to continue wasting time with a bunch of imbeciles or take early retirement and spend the remainder of his life in a rocking chair. The problem was … he could still remember the times when British soldiers were envied the world over.

The dilemma ended when he filled his lungs with air and grew at least three inches taller. "On the command 'atten-shun', you will bring your left foot up and place it firmly next to your right, except this time we will do it all together." He glared at each of us in turn, ensuring there was no misunderstanding. "I assume you all know your left from your right?"

The over-confident smiles failed to convince him so he repeated the question in a voice defying anything but a decisive 'yes' or 'no'. With a brief nod of satisfaction his chest came out once more. "Now at the same time as your feet move, bring those hands down to the sides of your leg, fingers slightly bent, thumbs in line with the seams of your trousers. Is that clear?"

The enthusiastic response encouraged him to proceed. "When I give the command, I want those left feet to come down so hard you can feel your balls vibrate." He ignored the sniggers. "Squad — wait for it, wait for it. Squad, ateeeeeeeen-shun!"

A multitude of left feet and a few delayed rights slammed into the concrete producing even more giggles as heads turned to locate the culprits.

"Stand still!" he bellowed, taking two steps forward, brass-ringed staff waving menacingly in our direction. "Keep those eyes to the front" We tried again and again but the clatter failed to improve, resulting in a few cracked skulls when the staff painfully reminded us this was no laughing matter.

"You are without doubt the worst fucking squad I have come across in twenty years! A disgrace to the army. I've seen rickshaw drivers with more brains than you lot and arthritic pensioners with better coordination."

For once the comparisons failed to produce the usual bout of giggles, although the odd smirk in no way endeared itself to a sergeant-major whose years of regimentation had plainly taken their toll on his patience.

"I'm glad you think it's funny. Let's see if you're still fucking smiling after ten laps of the square ... hands on heads." The bamboo staff smacked twice into the palm of his hand. "Anyone lowering their arms will get this up his arse."

The first few laps were easy, in fact we even discussed the possibility of being able to do more if necessary - a statement that began to look a little ambitious as the effort of trying to keep arms suspended left us gasping for breath long before the final circuit. We all managed to complete the task with the exception of a fifteen stone Geordie whose pained expression revealed something gold glistening from the vicinity of his first molar, bottom right. He completed eight laps, the last three at walking pace, and collapsed red-faced at the BSM's feet. Sergeant-Major Rhodes, sensing the dangers, tried desperately to move away, but his decision came too late as the foul smelling vomit erupted from the gunner's mouth, engulfing the officers' boots and trouser bottoms. The look of horror turned to disgust as he staggered back shaking each leg in turn, frantically trying to rid himself of the gooey mess.

"Dirty, filthy, bastard!" he screamed, advancing towards the unhappy Geordie who was crawling aimlessly around on hands and knees. "Look what you've fucking done!"

The first misplaced kick glanced off a hefty shoulder unlike the second, which thudded into the crouching body.

"Bastard!" continued the BSM, lashing out again and again with a soiled boot, each blow accompanied by a different obscenity - spat from a face no longer in control.

"Bloody hell, somebody stop him." The speaker decided it wasn't going to be him and remained unseen. "He'll kick him to death."

"The man's a fucking madman!"

"Do you think he's killed him?"

The concerns increased until half-a-dozen of us rushed forward, pulling the lifeless body away from any further punishment.

BSM Rhodes wanted to object but he could see the hostility on our faces and stepped back, though with no sign of remorse or concern as he pointed to his victim. "Take this man back to his billet let him sleep it off. He's lucky I'm not going to report him ... drunken bastard!" We left the blubbering Geordie to his room-mates and sauntered off to ponder this latest outburst of violence. As Leroy said "If that was meant to frighten us, it bloody well worked."

We suddenly began to see the army in a different light, never in a million years expecting the kind of violence witnessed since our arrival. If other national servicemen experienced similar ordeals they certainly never have discussed it otherwise more of an effort would have gone into avoiding bloody conscription. Remaining at home now looked a better alternative - no more parades, inspections or bullying, which seemed to be a regular occurrence at this particular camp.

In a way it was only made bearable by the slow growing comradeship of six very different young men thrown together in an attempt to overcome untidiness, lethargy, poor physical condition, cowardice and lack of ambition. I only suffered from two of these unlike some who would fail on all five.

The strict discipline combined with the much publicised 'bullshit' certainly didn't keep me awake at night or affect my performance during the day. Steve Clifford on the other hand found the whole twenty four hours stressful, not only outside the billet where his plummy voice and pompous manner made him an easy target, but also among fellow room-mates, who had no intention of making allowances for his privileged background.

People from different class structures rarely mixed well, each being suspicious of the other: one feeling superior; the other inferior. In a close environment the prejudices were even more in evidence, and that's how it was between Steve and the rest of us.

Difficult to say which class Jock Strachen came from but we assumed it wasn't the same as Steve when he called him a 'sanctimonious bastard' and displayed a definite tendency towards violence. His strong Scottish accent had an undertone of anger - turning a simple request into a demand. Steve thought he was a boxer on account of the powerful shoulders and short, thick neck, ideal for absorbing punches. He also smoked, cracked his knuckles, and interfered with himself, all of which annoyed Steve who said he would speak to him about them - but not yet.

Leroy Farley and Stan Clark were not only different in colour, but also in personality with Stan far more outgoing than the reserved cockney; capable of boring everyone to death with his knowledge of films and an ability to sound believable on subjects of which he had no experience. The gullible Lancashire postman, who originally considered national service a mere extension of the boy scouts, could spend hours perfecting his marching skills or preparing for inspection and still be reprimanded - unlike Leroy, who spent very little time doing either, but that was enough to make the inspecting officer feel inferior and sack his batman.

Gerry *'Timex'* Thomas, son of a village butcher, loved animals and therefore found himself at war with a father who made his living killing them. The family feud eventually forced him to seek his fortune in Swansea where he met the most important of his three passions, Wendy: the other two being wildlife conservation and his obsession with time. Even his hourly forecasts concluded with 'I wonder what she's doing now?'

If he wasn't describing her numerous qualities to anyone with an hour to spare, he would sit down and write page after page of drivel. Stan said he even explained the layout of the latrines and the intricacies of marching.

At the end of the day, with 'bullshit' forgotten, at least for a few hours, we would relax in our beds, encouraged by the darkness to join in the discussions, usually involving sex, drink and football. It seems we were experts on all three even if most of us had only experienced two. Occasionally there were other topics of conversation but no one could get really interested in governmental policies or the latest crime figures. Inevitably, well-rehearsed sexual exploits began to unfold, related with sufficient sincerity to make them believable.

"I'd be about ... seventeen," confirmed Stan. "She'd be about the same, but very well developed."

"Aren't they always?"

"Spitting image of Mitzi Gaynor. Did anyone see her in South Pacific, she took the part of Nellie—"

"Get on with it, for Christ sake!"

"Anyway, this one night when her parents were out we did it in front of the fire while the dog kept watch."

Jock's bed creaked as he turned on to his side. "You sure it wasn't with the dog while she kept watch?"

Stan glared at the Scotsman while he considered the point of continuing. "After that we used to do it every day in the shed. She used to scream and bang on the walls."

"But you still wouldn't let her out?"

"Oh, bollocks!"

"I remember this posh bird gave me a lift in a big, red Vauxhall Cresta ... leopard skin seat covers, nodding dog." Jock began to leer and you just knew it wasn't going to be another Romeo and Juliet. "She had a skirt up to her armpits, false eyelashes, and a habit of fondling the gear stick". He managed to sound suitably innocent. "Anyway she pulls up in this deserted lane and orders me into the back. 'Not bloody likely,' I said. 'I'm staying in the front with you.'"

Everyone agreed he'd made the right decision with the exception of Stan, who resolutely shook his head. "I would've gone in the back."

"What, and missed giving her a good shagging in the front?"

The laughter increased Stan's frown. "What's so bloody funny?"

Leroy had no intention of discussing his sexual awakenings, while Steve was, presumably, still waiting for it to happen.

Timex became highly indignant at suggestions he should reveal his first intimate moments with Wendy, reminding us in no uncertain terms 'it was none of our bloody business.'

I remembered only too well my catastrophic start to a life of unbridled passion, just about seven years before. Doreen lived next door - a real tomboy with ponytails, freckles and breasts that took a long time to develop. But when they did!

Suddenly I began to enjoy all the horseplay between us, the encounters became more physical, and in no time at all we were inspecting each others anatomical differences. I could never forget the feeling when I held those frightened breasts, or the heart stopping moment when her hands reached tentatively inside my trousers. Even though the process had been repeated with other women, that first time was always the one you remembered.

After weeks of mounting excitement as the caresses and kisses grew bolder, we were ready to take that final step. At least, she was. For some inexplicable reason I couldn't rise to the occasion. We blamed the weather, our surroundings, a faulty diet and finally each other. As the gulf between us widened, so did her impatience. Three weeks later she lost her virginity to a young electrician whose performance obviously wasn't dependent on anything. He only called to change a socket and in no time at all every socket in the house had been changed and she was pregnant.

I shared this experience with everyone in the billet, omitting one or two relevant facts and amending most of the others.

"I was lucky really," I concluded modestly, trying to portray a sense of gratitude. "We just happened to click. Trouble is she became obsessed ... wanted me all to herself ... but I wasn't ready to tie myself down to one woman."

When all the tales were told and all the lies listened to, we would snuggle down beneath the irritatingly, bristly blankets and dream of home. I thought of Wolverhampton with its hustle and bustle and familiar places. I would never want to live anywhere else, except perhaps Hawaii or Bermuda. What other town could offer top class football, horse racing, speedway, athletics, greyhound racing, a theatre, an art gallery, a newspaper and two breweries - in addition to the best looking girls who put their own interpretation on the slogan *We Do It Better*.

At times like these I thought about Ma, sitting quietly in her favourite chair staring aimlessly into space, thinking about Dad, me and all the other memories she clung to.

A woman's role in life hadn't changed much in fifty years. Working long, unrewarding hours, looking after a home and children who, sooner or later, would fly away, usually with anything they could lay their greedy little hands on. Caring for a husband who could easily be seduced by anyone in a skirt, by which time she was often too old for a new start. Worn out by the effort of it all, unable to compete against young women whose only responsibility was remembering to take the pill and deciding what colour knickers to wear. Sadly there was very little demand for a fifty-year-old woman who looked sixty, never complained and answered to the name of Rover.

Suddenly I had this overwhelming urge to do something special for Ma before it was too late. I would send her on a cruise, buy her that dream cottage by the sea complete with thatched roof and colourful window boxes, or I would get her the latest kitchen gadget. I made a mental note to check the price of electric can openers.

A lump came into my throat at the realisation I would probably be the last to know if anything unforeseen happened. I had this haunting picture of her collapsed in the green armchair clutching the Radio Times, unable to do anything but stare glassy-eyed at the wireless tuned in to the home service when her favourite programme had just begun on radio four.

She could still be in that position when the rent man called, or the milkman grew tired of picking his way through two dozen bottles of pasteurised. The tears began to fall: how would I ever pay for all that milk?

Chapter 5

A uniformed clerk, experienced in displaying authority without actually having any, bounded into the billet, sheet of paper in one hand, drawing pin in the other, and the impatient expression of someone who shouldn't really be doing this.

With complete disregard for the occupiers, he looked round for a suitable position to attach the notice, much to the annoyance of Jock who was busily engaged in a full-scale refurbishment of his toenails.

"Don't you buggers knock, or have you never heard of privacy?"

"Not since I've been in the army I haven't."

If the hostile reception bothered him, he didn't show it. Intent on pushing a drawing pin through the paper and into seasoned wood, the effort distorted his unmemorable features. The clerk stepped back, leaned forward to make a minor adjustment and then straightened up, nodding his approval at the near perfect alignment of the notice.

"What's all this about?" enquired Timex, glancing up briefly from his letter writing.

"Why, can't you read?"

"No he can't," Jock confirmed, pulling on the same pair of socks. "But you should see him tell the fucking time."

With an array of writing instruments at his disposal, the clerk selected an expensive looking fountain pen and tapped it lightly on the wall to attract our attention. "I'm afraid you've all been assigned to 'S' squad."

The expected outcry failed to materialise, just the puzzled expressions of ignorance.

"Surely you've heard of 'S' squad." The sea of faces remained blank. "Better known as the ... suicide squad."

The only response came from Jock's backside as he eased himself gently from the bed much to the clerk's disgust.

"I bet you won't do that with Sergeant Jenkins ... because that's whose squad it is."

Steve surprised everyone with his theatrical outburst. "My God, not THE Sergeant Jenkins?"

The clerk allowed himself a wry smile. "I thought that would get a reaction. Now you know what to expect."

"Who the hell's Sergeant Jenkins?" With each word the cigarette hanging limply from Jock's mouth bobbed up and down, depositing showers of ash onto highly polished boots as he struggled to fasten them. "Oh, fuck it!"

"Sergeant Jenkins is the bastard who runs the camp, assisted by the other two sadistic swine, Bombardier Hawkins and Lance Bombardier Dodds."

The tone of his voice suggested he had personal experience of all three. "They are without doubt the biggest bullies in the British Army and nobody … and I mean nobody … messes with them. They hate national servicemen, particularly if they are black or queer." He looked around for Leroy. "Sorry, mate, but that's how it is."

The tall, rangy black man shrugged his slim shoulders. "Don't worry. I've heard all the abuse before. We get used to it."

"It's not the verbal abuse you've got to worry about."

The clerk now had a captive audience, interested, but unsure of his motives. "It's the violence. They can make your life a bloody misery. At least half-a-dozen have committed suicide. That's why they call it the suicide squad."

"I've met nutters like these before."

Jock wasn't convinced. "Stand up to them and they'll soon back down."

"I'm telling you these are evil bastards. Their one aim in life is to break your spirit."

"They'd better not try it with me."

The clerk stared long and hard, as if deciding whether to waste any more time. "This isn't civvy street where you can run back home or complain to the police … it's the bloody army and there's sod all you can do about it. Anyway who are they going to believe? A snivelling little gunner or highly respected NCOs backed up by even higher respected officers?"

"But surely the officers don't condone such behaviour?" Steve's preconceived fear of violence began to look a distinct possibility as he sought some sort of reassurance. "After all they are in charge."

"Officers stay out of the way … so you won't get any help there. They all know what's happening but haven't got the guts to interfere. I think

Jenkins has some kind of hold over them, especially the CO." His voice dropped to little more than a whisper. "He's got a drink problem ... hardly surprising the number of parties they have over in the officers' mess." Another uneasy pause. "As a matter of interest you'll be under Captain Fosdyke, another spineless arsehole, so don't expect any help there."

This was hardly a calm, rational appraisal of army life and I wondered what his motives were.

"Why are you telling us?"

"I've only got three weeks of my national service left. Not much they can do to me now. You poor sods still have two years. I'm simply trying to warn you what to expect."

"Any more words of comfort or is it all doom and gloom?"

"Just one thing ... whatever you do, don't complain or put yourself in a vulnerable position."

His earlier offhand attitude was now one of concern. Even his facial expressions changed as he surveyed the room like a head prefect trying to locate a missing pencil.

"Stay out of their way whenever you can and keep this buttoned." A nail-bitten index finger skimmed over puckered lips. "And if you get half a chance of promotion, take it. If you feel like going AWOL, don't. They'll simply bring you back and really make you suffer." He backed nervously towards the door, pausing for a final comment. "Sergeant Jenkins will be coming to see you shortly so don't forget what I told you."

We were left with plenty to ponder, which in a way merely confirmed the physical assaults already witnessed were not just one-offs.

"Well, let's not get all morbid ... we'll just have to be careful". My attempt to make light of the situation failed to remove the apprehension circulating around the room.

"I never expected anything like this."

Steve stared long and hard at Leroy's downcast face. "I don't think any of us did."

"Well, you're the legal expert, there must be something we can do."

"Not unless you can prove it. Even then you would require witnesses."

"What about suicides, then?"

"Each one would have been thoroughly investigated. It is a crime for a person to aid or procure the suicide of another but proving it is very, very difficult."

"So what can we do?"

Their doleful expressions mirrored their fears. They weren't really soldiers - just young, innocent lads, plucked from a sheltered, comfortable life and dressed in soldier's uniforms.

"Look, we only have to put up with square bashing for a few weeks, then we'll be moved on. Surely we can stick it out that long."

I waited for a positive response, but the gloom remained.

"What about Saturday night? We'll be able to go out for a drink, place a bet, and check out the local talent."

"If they let us," argued Stan, determined to remain depressed. "You know what the clerk said."

Steve inadvertently managed to maintain the sombre mood. "I'm afraid neither gambling, drinking or chasing women appeals to me."

"Don't say you've never had a knee tremble?" Jock's lack of discretion brought much-needed colour to Steve's sallow complexion - in addition to widening his knowledge of slang euphemisms.

"I must admit it has never been one of my lifelong ambitions ... then, neither has playing football for England or knocking back ten pints."

Even before he opened his mouth you just knew Jock wasn't going to let the matter rest there. "Does that mean you're a bit ...?"

"Oh, I see. Just because I don't get drunk and throw up all over the place, or lust after anything in a skirt, I'm automatically classified as queer."

"Well, are you?"

"Does it make a difference?"

I could sense Steve's mounting frustration at being pushed into a corner. "Take no notice, mate. Your personal life is none of our business."

"It bloody is when we're living together."

Jock liked everything black and white, no secrets, and no disguises. If something needed saying, he'd say it. If it didn't need saying, he'd still say it. "I don't want to sleep next to a ..."

"It's the army he doesn't like, mate, not us."

"I know, that's what bothers me."

"See what I have to put up with." Steve felt deeply offended by the allegations, allowing his normally controlled exterior to briefly desert him. "Why can't you people mind your own bloody business, instead of interfering with others?"

Jock's expected retaliation failed to materialise. He satisfied himself with a sardonic smile as he turned away. It was all a game to the tough-talking Scotsman.

"Strange though ... having no interest in women." Stan directed his comments in my direction. "I met a nurse when I ended up in hospital." When no one enquired as to the reason for this emergency admission, he continued, "A real cracker. Dark hair, brown eyes, spitting image of Natalie Wood. She appeared in ..."

"Get on with it." came three voices, almost in unison.

"Anyway she got too serious ... wanted my ring, I'd only been out with her half-a-dozen times."

"I know what you mean, mate. My scoutmaster wanted the same thing. I hadn't been out with him at all."

The Lancashire postman wasn't listening, still reliving the tender moments in the casualty department. "When we parted it reminded me of that scene from *Love Is A Many Splendid Thing* when Jennifer Jones waves goodbye to William Holden. I can still see Jennifer now, tears trickling down her cheek."

"Yeah, some women will laugh at anything."

Stan continued his nostalgic ramblings, unconcerned at the limited interest. "Any minute now I expect William Hartnell to appear dressed as the sergeant, followed by Norman Wisdom, otherwise known as Private Pitkin. Has anyone seen *The Bulldog Breed?*"

"My uncle has one." Jock remembered the dog only too well. "Called it Winston."

"How original." mumbled Steve. "Every time you go there the little bugger either mounts your leg or rams his nose up your jacksie. My uncle used to say I got him too excited."

"What did you do?" enquired Steve, the hint of a smile already widening his mouth. "Dress provocatively or what?"

"No, I just used to wear a ... What the fucking hell does that mean?"

Before another meaningless argument broke out, the door burst open. In marched Bombardier Hawkins, eyes darting from left to right as the well-rehearsed feet echoed across the floor, coming to a thunderous rest with all the enthusiasm of a guardsman receiving the Victoria Cross. "Stand by your beds."

For twenty seconds we performed the panic version of musical chairs - only the bombardier's intervention brought the order to a satisfactory conclusion.

"Stand fucking still, what's the matter with you?"

"Sorry, bombardier."

"Shut up!"

"Sorry."

With three robot-like steps the fuming NCO had his staff firmly under the Welshman's chin. "If you open your mouth once more I'll ram this up your arse. Do you understand?"

Although ninety percent certain this was nothing more than an empty threat, events over the last few days had left Timex mistrustful of everyone, prompting a quick, and apparently acceptable nod.

An uneasy silence descended as we stood rigidly awaiting the arrival of Sergeant Jenkins, a position we maintained for thirty minutes. Only the movement of our eyes swivelling towards the door gave any indication we were still alive.

In contrast to the bombardier, he entered the billet quietly and calmly, stationing himself in a central position, jaw jutting forward, hands clasped tightly behind.

"I'm Sergeant Jenkins, in charge of 'S' squad. I think you all know Bombardier Hawkins."

A brief dip of the head introduced the scowling NCO.

"Our job is to instil things like discipline and respect, words you've probably never come across. You'll be with me for six weeks, at the end of which, assuming you survive ..." - the grin was clinical and never quite reached his eyes - "you'll be assessed and sent to where you can do the least damage."

Stan wanted to show he wasn't going to be intimidated. "I always fancied the parachute regiment, sergeant."

"All of them? Or one in particular?"

The Lancashire lad turned bright red, regretting his hasty interruption. "Er.... no. I mean I always fancied having a jump with the paras, sergeant."

"We all have our fantasies, gunner. Just don't let me find out about them."

Stan, aware of the smirks, tried a tactical diversion "Jock's attracted to dogs, sergeant."

"Well there's a couple of rough pubs in town." Locating the unfortunate Scotsman. "Just don't come back with any transmitted diseases … or I'll cut 'em off."

Jock's intended objection failed to escape his lips thanks to the eagle eye of Bombardier Hawkins. "Face the front."

The sergeant's head tilted slightly backwards, enlarging his eighteen-inch neck as he scrutinised each of us in turn. From the corner of my eye I saw him heading towards Timex, arms still clasped behind.

"And you are?"

The sergeant's unwavering gaze and intimidating stance appeared to affect the Welshman's ability to answer even the simplest question.

"Er...Er..."

"Out with it, lad. No good to the army if you don't know who you are."

With his brain otherwise engaged, Timex looked around appealingly for help, much to the bombardier's annoyance. "Eyes front. Answer the fucking question. It shouldn't be difficult, even for an imbecile."

"His name is Gerry … "

The surname died in mid-air as the bombardier's staff pushed into Leroy's neck. "Shut up, you black bastard. Nobody asked you."

Sergeant Jenkins acknowledged the reprimand with a satisfied nod, pushing his face closer to Timex. "I'm waiting."

You could almost smell the fear as the seconds ticked by then suddenly the words came tumbling out. "It's Gerry Thomas, sergeant"

The sighs of relief circulating round the room didn't come from either NCO, clearly annoyed at being denied the opportunity of satisfying their sadistic tendencies.

"Any good at writing, Thomas?"

Normally, we could all confirm his ability in that subject but wisely decided to let Timex speak for himself.

"Er... yes, sergeant."

"Then write your name a thousand times … just so you won't forget."

"Yes, Sergeant," replied the relieved Welshman, assuming his interrogation was at an end. "I'll get on to it right away."

"Just one more thing, Thomas. Get rid of that ring." He pointed to the gold encircled finger. "Give it to the bombardier. We can't have soldiers wearing jewellery."

Bombardier Hawkins offered the palm of his hand, aware of the slight hesitation. "I'm waiting."

Timex considered the alternatives which obviously failed to prove acceptable as he reluctantly acceded to the request. We all knew how much that would hurt him - the ring was a symbol of the love between him and Wendy.

"When do I get it back, sergeant?"

The question went unanswered as both NCOs closed in on Steve Clifford, struggling to remain calm as he prayed for a quick, uneventful interrogation.

"The name's Clifford, sergeant."

His eagerness to co-operate immediately backfired as the sergeant leant menacingly forward. "If I want your name, I'll ask for it."

"Yes, sergeant. Sorry, sergeant."

"Bit of a smart arse, aren't you, Clifford?"

Unsure of the context in which the comment was made, Steve decided to err on the side of caution. "No, sergeant."

Bombardier Hawkins jabbed the end of his staff under Steve's chin, forcing it up until his face was parallel to the ceiling. "If the sergeant says you're a smart arse, you are a smart arse. What are you?"

"A smart arse, bombardier."

Before further humiliations could be heaped upon the hapless gunner, Sergeant Jenkins stepped forward. "Tell me, Clifford. Why did you turn down the opportunity to become an officer?"

Steve remembered the clerk's warning but the prospect still didn't appeal. "I have no desire for promotion, sergeant."

"Prefer to start at the bottom with the men, eh, Clifford?"

"Yes, sergeant."

"Well don't let me find out. We can't have people like you corrupting young soldiers. Bad for morale, and makes them walk funny."

The sudden change in tone combined with the salacious inference prompted Steve to utter some form of protest, however feeble. "That's a little unfair, sergeant."

"If you think that's unfair, Clifford, you're in for a very rude awakening."

I knew the Bristol lad would be upset, having already voiced his fears regarding victimisation, but at least his humiliation was over for the time being.

"Name?"

"Stan, sergeant."

The unexpected reply widened the sergeant's eyes as he briefly glanced towards the bombardier and then back to his flustered prey.

"We're not on first name terms are we, gunner?"

"The man's a fucking moron, sergeant." The bombardier moved closer to Stan "What are you, gunner?"

"A fucking moron, bombardier."

"Well, now we've established what you are, answer the question."

"Er... I can't remember what it was, Bombardier."

"Your name, boy. We want your name."

"Oh, Clark, bombardier."

Sergeant Jenkins took over. "And what did you do for a living?"

Stan considered the sergeant's question knowing another mistake could mean a week confined to the latrines, or two weeks painting coal. But the delay merely provided the eager bombardier with an opportunity to demonstrate his prowess with the short staff. The polished wood made a resounding crack as it connected with Stan's unprotected skull, sending him reeling backwards, his face a mixture of pain and shock.

"Stand fucking still and answer the sergeant!"

Stan's eagerness to comply overcame his natural instinct to cower on the floor in a foetal position. He rose unsteadily to his feet, breathing heavily as he tried to recover. "I was ... a postman, sergeant."

"So this is about as smart as you get?"

Another nudge from the bombardier convinced him of the need to answer.

"Yes, sergeant."

"Think you can improve, gunner?"

"Yes, sergeant," replied Stan. His ruddy complexion gave him the appearance of an athlete, but only from the neck up. "Definitely."

I smiled at his gratitude, which couldn't have been more enthusiastic had he been offered a ten-pound note.

"You look pleased with yourself, Tramp."

"I'm just happy to be here, sergeant."

The bombardier moved alongside Sergeant Jenkins, his scowl increasing as he remembered our first meeting. "This is the bastard I told you about, sergeant. Troublemaker if ever I saw one."

"So you're the lad from Wolverhampton. Still, we all have our cross to bear. Last month we had one poor sod from Walsall." - exaggerated a shudder - "Makes your blood run cold just thinking about it."

"I bet you've never been to Wolverhampton, sergeant. It's full of characters."

"Yes I know, I read about them all the time." He remained unimpressed. "Robbers, rapists, crap football players..."

He wanted me to overstep the mark and so did Bombardier Hawkins, relishing another opportunity to display his skill with the staff.

"Wolverhampton has a lot to offer, sergeant."

"Yes I know. I've been offered some of it but I'm not that desperate." He turned to walk away, pausing for a final comment. "Do you have any more problems, gunner, apart from your mouth and place of origin?"

"I've got an undescended testicle, sergeant."

The bombardier's scowl creased his complexion, hands moving the wooden staff into a more accessible position. But the sergeant restrained him with a curt shake of the head.

"That shouldn't be a problem for long, gunner, you'll soon drop another bollock, and when you do..."

The unspoken threat received the bombardier's support as he paused to add his own contribution to my inescapable downfall. "Don't think you've got away with it, boy. It's just a matter of time"

They both converged on Jock with military precision, unable to hide their contempt for national servicemen, particularly Scottish ones. "You must be Strachan. I wondered when my luck would run out." Sergeant Jenkins glared around the billet, making it clear this was no laughing matter. "And how did you earn a living?"

Jock wasn't about to be intimidated, displaying a pair of clenched fists as evidence. "With these."

We all feared for the Scotsman, who seemed to find great difficulty respecting any form of authority, but the senior NCO remained calm, almost to the point of being interested.

"So what are you? A machinist? Concert pianist?"

"A doorman."

"Oh! And at which establishment did you provide this service? Claridges? The Dorchester? Savoy?"

"Macgregor's night club in Glasgow. I threw out any bastard who couldn't behave."

"With those?" suggested Sergeant Jenkins pointing down to the

Scotsman's hands.

"That's right." Jock's confidence began to rise as he displayed a pair of clenched fists. "With these."

Retribution was swift and painful. Even the Scotsman's face expressed surprise before changing to agony as the bombardier's staff smashed against his knuckles three times in succession.

"Quick thinking, bombardier."

"Oh I could see what he had in mind, sergeant ... threatening you like that with his fists."

"Good job you were there to defend me."

"That's what happens when you try to be friendly, sergeant. I think he should be reported," suggested Bombardier Hawkins, unconcerned as Gunner Strachan performed some form of tribal dance accompanied by the occasional reference to Jesus Christ.

The sergeant waited patiently for the pain to subside while he considered the possibility of inflicting further punishment. "Raising your fists against an NCO is a very serious offence, gunner. One that should undoubtedly be reported. However, on this occasion I am prepared to overlook it."

Bombardier Hawkins shoved his face close to Jock's sweating features. "You're a very lucky bastard, boy. What are you?"

We all expected fireworks, having frequently been impressed by his so-called hard man image. But either the pain, or fear of another onslaught, turned him into a bit of a damp squib. "A lucky bastard, bombardier."

"Louder, we can't hear you."

A long pause suggested he may not co-operate but the defiance, in common with his credibility, suffered another humiliation. "A lucky bastard, bombardier."

With Jock's reputation left in tatters they approached Leroy, eyeing him from head to foot and back again as the beads of perspiration began to form on his ebony features.

"What's your name?"

"Farley, sergeant."

"And what menial task did you do in civvy street? Carry cases? Wait on tables?"

Bombardier Hawkins silently congratulated the sergeant with a brief nod, adding his own line of sarcasm. "Probably never worked in his bloody life."

"A fireman with the London Fire Brigade, been there ..."

"Just answer the question, we don't want fucking speeches." Leroy's faultless appearance and immaculate display of equipment infuriated both NCOs, who responded by demolishing all of his hard work.

"Not good enough, gunner."

"Fucking disgrace," confirmed the bombardier, each word emphasised with a vicious jab on the forehead. "Still, what can you expect when they're not used to the white man's ways"

I feared for Leroy as the taunts continued, the sergeant's voice remaining at one level, unlike the crazy bombardier whose melodious tones went up and down the scales. However, the black face stayed impassive, only the eyes giving any indication of his anger.

"If this mess isn't rectified in fifteen minutes ..." The unfinished sentence gave Bombardier Hawkins the opportunity to conclude the outcome. " ... you, boy, will be back shining fucking shoes."

The room remained quiet long after their disappearance; the kind of uncomfortable silence you recalled as a schoolboy after being shown up in front of the whole class.

"Perhaps tomorrow will be a better day," I suggested optimistically. But no one really believed me.

Chapter 6

The increasing brutality, initially accepted as part of the toughening up process had now become a real problem - each of us at some time had to endure physical violence for the most trivial of reasons. A look, however innocent, would be described as insolent and penalised with extra duties, while a word out of place guaranteed at least twenty laps of the parade ground carrying a 56lb shell. Even an item of cutlery not perfectly aligned became an excuse for some form of punishment. More serious offences gave Sergeant Jenkins and his henchmen the opportunity to administer their own form of retribution - usually involving a hard wooden instrument or a clenched fist.

Beatings were carried out as so-called acts of self-defence in answer to our aggressive behaviour. Apparently the cracked ribs of Gerry Thomas were sustained when the mild-mannered Welshman became violent and had to be forcibly restrained. Leroy's broken nose and battered features occurred during a lesson in unarmed combat, witnessed by two NCOs and a lieutenant who wasn't even present. In addition we had the constant humiliation - particularly upsetting for Steve and Leroy, who were easy targets.

However, the biggest casualty of all had to be Timex - unprepared for inspections, uncoordinated on parade, and a disaster on the sports field. "I can't put up with much more of this." His stiff upper lip, under pressure from day one, now began to look decidedly limp as he worried about Sergeant Jenkins, NCOs and the contents of Wendy's brief letter.

"There's something wrong here," he exclaimed, reading the letter he had received more than a week before. "It just doesn't make sense."

"Grammar was never my strong point, either." Jock's confession held no surprises. "Is it the spelling or what?"

Timex straightened from his slouching position, usually a sign someone with authority was in the vicinity. "I'm not bothered about the bloody English, it's what she says that bothers me. If I could just talk to her, find out what the problem is."

"You'll be able to telephone her on Saturday." Steve's optimism failed to take into account another problem facing the Welshman.

"Aren't you forgetting we're all confined to camp except these two jammy bastards?"

I grinned, unlike Stan who suddenly felt guilty. "I could give her a ring for you."

"What bloody good would that do?"

Stan couldn't immediately think of any advantage. "I could pass a message on ... tell her how much you love her and can't wait to give her a good shafting."

Stan realised his mistake when a size ten boot flew at him followed by its owner, intent on extracting an apology. Only Steve's repeated appeals convinced Timex of the importance of removing his hands from around Stan's throat.

"Did you see that?" whispered Leroy, sitting cross-legged beside me. "I think poor old Gerry's at the end of his tether. I don't think he can take this kind of treatment."

I wasn't quite sure which kind he meant but I had to agree with his diagnosis. "He's certainly finding things difficult. Having said that, it's not exactly a picnic for you either."

He shrugged off the concern, large brown eyes warning against pursuing the matter. "I'm used to it."

He moved away, while I reflected on the exceedingly slow passage of time, which in turn reminded me of a holiday in sunny Majorca when the daytime temperature never dipped below 95 degrees, prompting the majority of hotels to offer free beer. Unfortunately, neither Clare nor I could take advantage of either thanks to an outbreak of sickness and diarrhoea which confined us to the bathroom for six horrendous days. When we eventually appeared, looking pale and gaunt, the staff gave us a round of applause and a certificate for the *sexiest couple of the month*.

Thoughts of that holiday soon passed into history, as did our first weeks of bullshit.

Suddenly, Saturday was upon us in a blaze of glory. The late Autumn sun forced its way through slow moving cotton-wool clouds; seagulls wheeled overhead uttering their raucous cries, and a tea-stained letter arrived, addressed to Private Tramp - its half open flap crushing any hope of receiving financial assistance.

Steve's letters were always typed by his father's secretary and signed by her in his absence. Hardly the kind of father-son relationship most lads took for granted. Even the contents lacked warmth; usually confined to the latest courtroom battles or legislative document - neither of which would help Steve in his battle for survival.

Although letters from home were always welcome, they hardly curled your toes with excitement. For example, Stan's correspondence normally contained news of at least one death with the possibility of others in the pipeline. In addition, he had to suffer the embarrassment of being reminded to dry between his toes and wear clean underwear in case of an accident.

The official looking posts Jock received were either companies demanding repayment of a loan, or the tax man, concerned about his lack of co-operation since leaving school.

"No letter again, Leroy?"

"Doesn't look like it, Joe. Maybe tomorrow," he replied, offering no explanation about who or where it might come from.

My grubby envelope containing two recognisable pages of works paper complete with punched holes for filing certainly had me guessing. Who from work would be interested in my welfare? I started to read:

Dear Joe,

How are they treating you, mate? Is all that regimentation getting you down? I know exactly how you feel - I once spent two weeks at Butlins.

The lads in the tool room send their regards, all except Ron Bishop. He says you still owe him tea money, coupon money and your share towards the last works outing. Paul Langford's in trouble again, this time for punching the foreman. Apparently he put a stop to the card school just when Paul had a prile of aces. The manager wanted Paul sacked, but the union said he was fully justified in his actions and threatened an all-out strike. Thankfully the management saw sense and apologised to Paul with an assurance to sack the foreman upon his return from hospital.

Do you remember Tommy Baker who worked in the stores? Little skinny bloke, never looked well. He died suddenly last week leaving a wife and two dozen racing pigeons. She's alright but the pigeons are pining. Nobby still pops to see if there's anything she wants, and if there is he gives it to her, except now he doesn't have to wait until Tommy's on nights.

Don Carter's blackouts are getting worse, yesterday he passed out carrying the breakfasts. He was alright but the toast was cold. We've begged him to see a doctor, otherwise the same thing could happen when he's fetching the dinners. Your old mate

Barry Turner's finally got a yes from Marlene Drew. He wanted you as best man until he found out she'd said yes to you three months earlier. Fortunately, no one told him about the abortion. However, he is still secretary of the gun club so I should be very careful if you come home on leave.

Well that's about all for now.

Best wishes,

Harry.

P.S If you could forward the money it comes to three pounds. You know what a big mouth Ron Bishop has?

I screwed the paper into a ball and tossed it casually towards the locker, dismissing any thoughts of a reply. The only letters of interest to me now were those expressing thoughts of love. Unfortunately, they too had become a little stereotyped, as pointed out by one young lady who replied - *Dear Joe, thank you for the circular.*

By seven o'clock Saturday evening, the expressions separated who would be going out from those confined to a night of high jinks and revelry washing out the latrines.

"I feel lucky tonight." Obviously no-one else shared my enthusiasm. "Maybe I'll meet the girl of my dreams, fall in love and live happily ever after."

"Hoping to get your first shag, then?"

Jock proved once again that he wasn't big on romance; preferring the more direct approach. I ignored the cynicism, beckoning my colleague for the evening towards the door.

"Stanley, let you and me go and paint the town red."

"What a good idea, Olly."

The impression of Laurel and Hardy lost a little of its impact in the translation - but we both enjoyed it.

After great deliberation, disregarding the cheaper price of beer and close proximity to a fish and chip shop, we chose the Dog and Duck pub, swayed by its picturesque appearance portraying a typical black and white timber-framed building from the 17th century. Sadly the olde worlde charm didn't extend beyond the entrance, already awash with someone's dinner.

Within seconds, every eye in the bar turned in our direction, decided we were unimportant, and rejoined the clamour of voices trying to attract the barmaid's attention.

"What do you want, Joe?"

"Pint of bitter, mate. Never touch anything else."

"I'm a cider man."

"Yes, I thought you might be."

"And what does that mean?"

"Nothing ... just making conversation."

We headed for the bar using a combination of body swerves and side steps that would have made Stanley Matthews proud - even if one or two of the regulars weren't.

"Look where you're bloody going!" - "Who do you think you're fucking pushing?"

Three *excuse me's* and an apologetic *sorry*, squeezed us in at the bar, almost within touching distance of the elderly barmaid, ageing even more rapidly as the effects of trying to serve a dozen jostling customers began to melt her makeup.

She directed her frustration at Stan. "Can't you see I'm busy? I've only got one pair of hands."

"I only asked for a couple of drinks." he mumbled to no-one in particular, unable to hide the embarrassment of being singled out.

"Take no notice, mate. She's just cranky because the brewery renovated everything but her."

The recently cropped former postman located the clock, nodding each time the second hand moved. "Reminds me of the film, *High Noon*, starring Gary Cooper. He finished that film in 1952, winning 'best actor' award. I bet you don't know when he finished 'Sergeant York."

"I didn't even know he'd been in the army, mate."

"He finished Sergeant York in 1940 and won an award. If he'd come and finish off Sergeant Hawkins, we'd give him a bloody medal."

I looked away before he could continue the pointless discussion. At least it took my mind off the clock - I didn't think I could stand a time check every five minutes.

"Seven forty... two." He gave me a nudge when I didn't respond. "Seven forty two."

"Yes, I heard you the first time. Just because Timex is without a watch doesn't mean you've got to take his place. He used to send everyone mad with his bloody time checks."

He winked mischievously and I knew it would be bad news. "He's got another one arriving any day, but don't tell anyone."

"Not even Lance Bombardier Dodds?"

"He's the bastard who smashed his last one."

"Oh, right. Let's hope no one tells him about this one, then."

Eventually help arrived behind the bar, accompanied by wolf whistles and a round of hearty applause. She was about twenty, an inch over five foot with long black hair swept away from her face and held in a ponytail by an elastic band. She played down her attractive looks by wearing functional clothes and very little makeup, but when she smiled the whole room seemed to light up and suddenly I was in love.

"Spitting image of Elizabeth Taylor … just a bit slimmer." Stan let out a sigh, staring wistfully across the bar. "I can name every film she's ever made."

I thought of ways to avoid another lesson on Hollywood stars - but nothing less than a ferret up his trousers would stop him now.

"Lassie Come Home 1942; National Velvet 1944; Father of the Bride 1950; Giant 1956; Raintree County 1957; and Cat on a Hot Tin Roof 1958, one of the last films I saw prior to being called-up."

I wondered if he would question me on the history of Elizabeth Taylor, but he realised I wasn't really listening.

"You needn't bother looking all goggle-eyed. She'll not want anything to do with the likes of us."

He was wrong.

"Hi, I'm Julie," she said. "What can I do for you two lads?"

I resisted the urge to tell her and extended my hand. "I'm Joe Tramp and this is Stan, my batman."

"I'm not a bloody batman."

She patted his hand reassuringly, dismissing the anger before it could fester. "I know, you look more like an officer to me. Now what can I get you to drink?"

While Stan entertained the young lady with his knowledge of ciders, I studied her satin, smooth complexion, only a shade darker than pale, just light enough to reveal the tiniest freckles on her face and neck. She had the fullest lips, with bright, twinkling eyes and the most perfect teeth. Crooked ones always gave me a grim reminder of the penalty I paid for French kissing Gillian Cartwright. I never realised how painful a metal brace could be until she pushed me hurriedly away. I couldn't talk for a month and so I became a silent hero at school. Ma told the police someone tried to cut my tongue out, sending them on a search for a tall dark man carrying a knife.

The hunt ended when I picked out the inspector at an identity parade.

Eventually the drinks appeared, served with a smile she struggled to maintain as Stan went through his pockets.

"I'll come back for the money." she said.

Her trust failed to impress an old man with a permanent sniff and overgrown eyebrows. "Don't let the buggers get away with it ... they get plenty of money nowadays." Murmurs of agreement echoed along the bar. "Now when I was in the army things were different. We had to live on five bob a week."

"Still do don't you, Sam?" The comment produced peels of raucous laughter, returning Sam to his beer and memories of the time you could buy a drink, a packet of cigarettes and still have enough left out of a shilling to turn the head of a young gal.

With the care of a pensioner paying out the last of his savings, Stan placed exactly the right amount on the bar while Julie served someone else, smiling coyly at a flattering remark, or wagging a warning finger at an over-familiar customer. I decided she probably flirted with everyone and turned away to watch Stan who was now on the dartboard. At least that shouldn't get me too excited, particularly as it soon became clear his lack of eye and arm coordination were not confined to the parade ground.

I declined an offer to partner him, preferring to rejoin the other voyeurs in their silent seduction of the pretty barmaid.

You could almost see their minds going back to a time when they too were young and virile. Now the hair was reduced to a few carefully positioned strands, and teeth had been replaced by ill-fitting dentures, distorting the use of any word containing the letter 's'. In those days sex was new and exciting - anytime, anywhere, not once in a blue moon with a partner who said 'not again'.

"Can I get you another drink?" Julie's smile defied you to refuse, dismissing any thoughts of becoming a teetotaller.

"Er.... yes, same again, and have one yourself."

"Thanks, I'll have a Babycham now the rush is over."

We chatted about all manner of things and after twenty minutes I knew we were meant for each other. Even the star signs were compatible; something she felt strongly about. Naturally, I confessed to having great faith in the astrological powers until she confirmed nothing would be rising for the next seven or eight months. I considered explaining it had risen every morning for the past seven days, and so had everyone else's in the billet, but I didn't think she would understand. Most mornings you couldn't see anyone's face unless you stood on a bed.

As the conversation flowed and my courage increased, it was simply a matter of time before I made a subtle approach. "How about you and I getting together one night?"

"What are you going to do about your friend?" she replied, staring over my shoulder.

"Oh, he can stay in and press my uniform."

"No, I mean now. He appears to be in a spot of bother."

I turned to see Stan protesting meekly as a beefy fellow in a black T-shirt poked him repeatedly in the chest. For some reason he disliked northerners, particularly if they reminded him of George Formby - unlike Stan who confessed to liking everyone south of Manchester. This diplomatic approach merely encouraged the unshaven and probably unwashed man in black to take even more liberties with a couple of stinging slaps across the face from a muscular tattooed arm.

"Don't keep backing away," I yelled sensing his fear. "Hit him in the stomach ... it's big enough."

Stan fended off another wild swing, almost stumbling in his attempt to get away. "I don't want any trouble."

I pushed him back to his feet. "That's OK then, you're not giving him any."

The big man gave another shove, the effort reddening his piggy eyes. "Come on, you bastard, stand and fight ... or are you chicken?"

"No he's not," I responded, knowing how modest the Lancashire postman could be. "He just takes a long time to warm up."

"We don't want you bastards in here."

"We were just leaving weren't we, Joe?"

"Were we buggery! I've just ordered another round."

"I'm going to pass out."

"Not for another four weeks you're not."

As if to prove me wrong, his legs began to buckle and down he went, along with two stools and a pint of cider. As a final humiliation, an overflowing ashtray landed on his face, followed by the fluttering contents mingling with blood, sweat and cider.

"You mad sod," I yelled, straightening up. "Now look what you've done."

"I never fucking touched him."

I kicked the heavy glass ashtray under the bar. "Not half you didn't, just look at the state of him."

Half-a-dozen faces peered over, anxious to express their concerns.

"He's covered in blood."

"I don't think he's moving."

"Is he dead?" asked the old man with the snotty nose, not really bothered one way or another.

The assailant gingerly retreated from the hostile glances. "I told you … I never fucking touched him."

I bent lower, hastily spreading the blood over his face. "Looks like he'll need an ambulance … might even require plastic surgery."

All eyes focused on the black-vested attacker, sweating more than ever as he shuffled backwards towards the door. "It's a fucking set-up."

With one last desperate glance around, he disappeared, at the same time as Stan's eyelids flickered open.

"What happened?"

"It's alright," whispered Julie, gently dabbing the blood with a reddening towel. "We've already sent for the police. Just lay still."

"The police?" He pushed Julie's hand away and sat upright, brushing off the flakes of ash. "But I haven't done anything wrong." Without another word he shot to his feet, oblivious to the concerns as he fled from the pub, protesting his innocence.

"Don't you think you should go after him?" Julie paused for a reason, right hand resting lightly on my arm. "A blow on the head can do a lot of damage. He probably doesn't even know what he's doing."

"No change there then."

I wanted to pursue our friendship, not chase after lunatics. But it wouldn't do any harm to show a little compassion. "You're right! I'll go and find him, make sure he's alright. Sorry, I have to rush off."

My reluctance to leave didn't go unnoticed.

"I'm sorry, too," she said, "but at least you know where I am most evenings."

Her parting words removed much of the anger directed at Stan for cramping my style, enabling me to display a limited amount of sympathy as I quickly reduced the gap between us.

"How are you feeling, mate?"

"How do you expect me to feel?" He waited for me to draw level and then his pace returned to normal. "I'll tell you one thing ... we shan't be going back there again, at least I won't."

"Why not?"

He slowed again. "Why not? Why bloody not? I'd be the laughing stock of the pub, that's why not."

"I didn't see anyone laughing. In fact they were quite impressed."

"Impressed? Bloody impressed? What at, the speed I pissed off?"

I tried to look suitably confused, finding difficulty in matching his ever changing pace. "He was the one who pissed off. We all assumed you shot outside to teach him a lesson. That's what you said on the way out."

"I said that?"

"Don't you remember, mate? The way you went after him had us all worried. 'Where's the bastard gone?' you kept shouting. 'When I catch up with him, I'll kick the crap out of him.'"

A slight smirk tugged the corners of his mouth as he stopped completely. "I must've been angry."

"Angry's not the word. Good job you didn't catch up with him, that's all I can say."

"I suppose it is." The smirk enlarged as he set off once more, this time with a definite purpose in his stride. "I might have done a lot of damage. The trouble is I'm a slow starter."

"Yes, I noticed. One bloke said he'd never seen such control, just like watching Alan Ladd in action."

He liked the comparison, glancing around with a challenging expression. "I never looked at it that way."

"You don't see James Cagney throwing his weight around"

The doubt returned as his pace slowed and I wondered if they were in some way connected. "I'm not surprised, he's not much more than a fucking midget."

We continued in silence, ignoring the smell of chips and the professional smile of a bored-looking prostitute - shoulders back, chest out in an attempt to convince male passers-by their money would guarantee complete satisfaction. When I glanced back she was removing traces of newly applied lipstick from her teeth with a pinkish tongue, body slumped, almost as though someone had switched her off.

We arrived back at the billet, Stan eager to display his injuries and no doubt explain their cause.

"What the..." He stopped abruptly, leaving me to peer over his shoulder at the chaos inside. Beds overturned, blankets strewn across the floor and all the lockers upended - their contents poking out from beneath. Only the table appeared untouched, unlike the lads, battered and bruised as they stood forlornly around.

"What happened?"

"Don't ask me." Jock looked briefly in my direction, continuing to shake his head. "I've only just come in."

I approached Timex, swollen face reducing the size of his eyes, struggling to fight back the tears. I wanted to reassure him with a comforting arm but men didn't do that. "Are you alright, mate?"

He tried answering with a smile, except the split lips made even that gesture painful, so I touched his arm to show I understood. Leroy too exhibited the effects of someone's fists, unlike Steve, whose boyish features remained intact, only the clenched hands across his midriff gave any indication of where his ordeal had taken place.

"Who did this?"

Leroy tried to laugh it off but it was a meaningless expression so he gave up. "You should see the state of the opposition."

Steve practised a number of deep breaths, grimacing with each one. "Hawkins and his band of merry men ... merry, as in drunk. What could we do against half-a-dozen?"

I wanted to suggest a few things, including fighting back or even running away, except now wasn't the time for post-mortems.

"What was it all about?"

Leroy made sure his cheekbones were in the right position before offering a reply. "They burst in accusing us of bullying, saying they would teach us a lesson. That was it. They just got on with it. At one stage I thought Hawkins would kill Gerry, I really did."

"He's a sadistic animal with psychopathic tendencies," decided Steve. I imagined him standing up in court saying the same thing.

"There was no remorse, no concern, just this crazy look in his eyes."

"Wish I'd have been here." Stan fingered his injury, trying to think what difference it would have made.

"Even the odds up a bit." Gerry spoke out for the first time, emotion clearly showing as his Welsh voice grew higher. "This can't be right, Joe, having to put up with this kind of treatment."

"It's like being prisoners-of-war." The warning glances dissuaded Stan from comparing us to real heroes. "Only not so...bad."

"What do you think we should do Joe?"

I cast a meaningful look in Jock's direction, wanting to remind him who the bouncer was. But even he didn't have the answer.

"First thing we do is tidy this place. Won't take long if everyone gets stuck in. Then a visit to the MO. Get these injuries attended to. That way we'll be down on record ... which may come in useful later."

"What about complaining?"

The ruddy-faced conscript with the ashtray size gash, who never faced anything more sinister than a Yorkshire terrier in five years of posting letters, waited for an answer.

"Complaining isn't going to work, mate. They'll always have enough witnesses or evidence to put themselves in the clear. Our word against theirs? I don't think so. Anyway, who would we complain to? The officers are a joke, at least the ones we've come across are. They seem more afraid of Jenkins and his mob than we are."

"We could write to the papers ... tell people back home."

I thought about the lads at work, and everyone who survived their two year call - each with an exaggerated account of bullying and bullshit. "They'd think we couldn't take it, frightened of being picked on." I looked at the disappointed, battle-scarred faces, knowing I wasn't being particularly encouraging. "If we stick together ... watch out for each other ... we'll get through it."

"What about all those suicides the clerk mentioned, all from this squad." Steve's concern overcame any legal requirement for sticking to the facts. "They can't all be a coincidence."

"I think what the bastards do is try to isolate people, especially the vulnerable, that's why we have to be on our guard."

"I can't take much more of this! If it continues I'm going AWOL, before they finish me altogether." Timex said what most of the others thought, obviously looking for me to come up with the solution.

Chapter 7

Sunday mornings conjured up visions of breakfast in bed listening to the local Salvation Army band butchering *Onward Christian Soldiers*. Somewhere between verses three and four signalled the arrival of uniformed collectors, trained to smile as they were told to 'piss off.' Ma always contributed, ensuring a return visit and the satisfaction of knowing she was providing food and shelter for an endless assortment of spongers. A brief glance through the War Cry and I would be off to sample Banks's bitter, and get a chance to hear how the country really should be run. Four pints later, I would be heading home, wondering why at least three of the pub regulars weren't in the cabinet.

Roast beef, Yorkshire pudding and home-made apple pie, washed down with a mug of hot tea sweetened with condensed milk, usually had the desired effect, and I would sleep until the smell of thickly buttered toast found its way into my nostrils.

But that was before.

Now our day of rest began at 5:30 a.m. Each morning heralded another round of parades, inspections and verbal abuse. Breakfast lacked the basic ingredients like eggs and bacon although beans were in plentiful supply, ladled out by a former lorry driver whose experience of transport cafes earned him a posting to the catering corps.

"Bloody beans again," moaned Jock, inspecting the contents with all the concern of a biologist discovering mould on his porridge. "You can't win a war on beans."

"No, mate, but you can sound as though you're winning."

I declined second helpings, suggesting everyone did the same in order to reduce the nightly sound effects.

Eventually Timex joined Jock and me, his bruised face and glum expression focused on the plate of beans he deposited on the table. "If they thin this out any more we'll be able to drink it."

His Welsh voice no longer went up and down the scales and it was clear to see how much the past weeks had taken out of him.

"How did you get on with the MO, mate?"

"Alright." I waited for further information but he appeared more interested in moving his beans into military formations.

"You told him what happened last night?"

Timex sat in silence, only the slow rising blush giving any indication he was listening.

"You didn't tell him, did you?"

"You said not to complain."

"Oh, for Christ's sake! You had the ideal opportunity to do something about it ... you and Leroy."

"We were going to."

"Then why didn't you?"

"Dodds was there."

"So?"

"He warned me about saying anything ... said he'd make my life a misery"

"Well he's doing that anyway." Jock couldn't hide his disgust, not that he ever really tried. "What did you tell the MO? You'd beaten yourself up?"

"Dodds told him Leroy and I had been fighting. He said we were lucky not to be on a charge."

Not for the first time, my anger threatened to vent itself on the Welshman. But the real culprits were the army. Bullying and violence of any kind were totally alien to Timex, and yet he found himself in an occupation that openly promoted both.

"Nothing we can do about it now, mate. You'll just have to be more careful in future."

"What future?"

His response couldn't have been more depressing had I presented him with a do-it-yourself castration kit. However, unlike me, Jock wasn't ready to extend the hand of sympathy.

"Any word from...what's her name?"

"You know very well there isn't. And her name is Wendy."

"Probably a good reason," I added, unsure whose side I was on.

"Yeah, she's found some other bugger."

I gave the Scotsman a warning glance but he wasn't about to let the Welshman off lightly. "Let's face it, you're no Tony Curtis."

Timex fingered the bruises, trying to decide if the reference was before or after. "I can't bloody help it."

"You shouldn't have beaten yourself up."

Whether it was Jock's comment, or the laugh at the end, I couldn't be quite sure - but one of them certainly sparked an outburst.

"It's just a bloody game to you. You don't give a sod about anything." Timex stood up, bracing himself on the table in readiness for another round of insults, but the cheers changed his mind and he immediately sat down, embarrassed by the attention. "Wait until you meet the right one … you won't be laughing then."

"And don't I know it. Nothing like a woman to wipe the smile off your face. You're a perfect example of that. Why don't you forget about her and enjoy yourself? I bet that's what she's doing"

"No she's not."

"How do you know?"

Timex's body seemed to deflate. He wasn't sure about anything any more. Even his voice lacked conviction as it dropped a couple of octaves. "She has no reason to."

Jock's sympathy wasn't about to surface just yet. "She's bound to be feeling frustrated, and you're not there to give her one."

The Welshman realised, not for the first time, why he preferred animals to people. "She wouldn't do anything behind my back." It was difficult to distinguish between a statement or question. "She's not like that."

"They're all like that," sneered the cynical Scotsman. "Tell him, Joe."

"Probably the ones you know are. Timex obviously trusts her."

"Yeah, that's right. I do." He sounded far more positive as the doubts began to recede. "Because I know she loves me."

Nobody had ever loved Jock. At three months his mother left him with a neighbour while she went to the pictures. By the time she returned, the cinema had been replaced by a swimming baths and he was in secondary school. In the meantime his father incurred the wrath of the law by trying to swap him for a greyhound. His unsettled childhood no doubt accounted for his negative attitude towards relationships.

"What's love got to do with anything? It's all about getting what you can and then moving on before it buggers your life up." The embittered Scotsman, no longer smiling, rose quickly and moved to another table leaving Timex a mixture of confusion and frustration.

"He doesn't know what he's talking about, the bastard!"

"Then don't worry about him."

"I'm not. The bastard!"

I remained silent, knowing sooner or later he would reopen the discussion and I knew what the topic would be.

"We made such promises, Joe."

"Well I'm sure she meant them at the time."

"So you think the same as him?"

"Look, mate, you've got enough to worry about here, without further distractions. You've had your watch smashed, personal belongings either destroyed or confiscated, on top of which they've knocked you from pillar to post. It's all about survival, mate, and somehow you've got to get through this."

"That's easier said than done, Joe." He leaned across the table, elbows either side of his plate. "I wouldn't admit this in front of the others, but these NCOs terrify me."

I resisted the urge to tell him most of the camp were aware of the fact. "Nothing to be ashamed of, mate. Plenty more here who feel the same as you."

"I only have to see them coming towards me and I break into a cold sweat. Hardly the way for a grown man to behave."

"I think most of the lads are frightened of Sergeant Jenkins." I wanted to exclude myself, but it sounded like bravado. "So you're not alone there. Just remember we're all on your side ... even Jock."

"He's got a bloody funny way of showing it."

"We all cope differently. Jock gives the impression he couldn't care a toss but he gets worried and maybe a little scared at times ... the same as we all do. Stan loses himself in old films, takes his mind off other things. Leroy takes his frustration out on his kit, that's why it's better than anyone else's ... while Steve retreats into his shell, wishing he'd spent more time in the gym and less in the classroom. He might have qualifications, but they don't count for bugger all in here."

Timex continued rocking backwards and forwards, fascinated by the fart-like sounds emitting from the chair. When he paused in the forward position, I feared a resumption of his troubled love life.

"What about you, Joe? Things don't get you down like they do the rest of us."

"That's the benefit of a misspent youth, mate. You always come across scum like these ... then it doesn't come as a complete shock."

67

The slight exaggeration on my part fortunately went unchallenged although no doubt I could have furnished him with sufficient information to maintain my streetwise credibility. "One day you'll look back on all of this and laugh."

"I haven't found much to bloody laugh at so far."

I nudged his elbow, nodding briefly towards the door. "I think that could change any minute."

The bespectacled young lieutenant had inexperience written all over him. It proved to be an accurate assessment as he faltered at the sight of two dozen gunners anticipating the arrival of a seasoned duty officer - one with self-assurance and authority. Lieutenant James had neither, as previously pointed out to him by a drill instructor who nicknamed him 'Jessie'. He had haemorrhoids, bladder problems and a tendency to stutter in times of adversity, any one of which should have kept him out of national service. Unfortunately, they failed to appear during the medical, delaying his progress up the accountancy ladder by two years.

He approached the cook with a smile, ignoring the advice of a senior officer who warned against the dangers of over-familiarity with the lower ranks. "Good morning cook, what's on the menu today?"

The unsmiling ex-lorry driver, whose only claim to fame centred on his record of never having used the word 'sir' in six months, glanced down at the solitary metal pot three quarters full of beans and wondered why the lieutenant didn't do the same. "It's all in there."

Lieutenant 'Jessie' James adjusted his glasses and leant forward. "Good solid food, that's what the men want." He bent lower over the pot trying to think why - making a failed grab for his spectacles as they fell silently into the beans. "Oh, bugger!"

The cooks' expression didn't alter as he fished them out, allowing the beans to slide off prior to a brief rinsing under the tap. He handed them back as though it were a daily occurrence, ignoring the acknowledgement and ensuing clatter as the officer's stick fell to the floor.

"Oh, bloody bugger!" Lieutenant James gave up on the glasses, shoving them into a breast pocket while he waited for someone to retrieve his stick. When it didn't happen he considered issuing an order. But his nerve failed. In one rapid movement he grabbed the stick, allowing the cap to slide forward obscuring his vision. "Oh, bloody buggering bugger it!"

With his colour rivalling the beans, he made a few hurried adjustments before allowing himself the privilege of a sheepish grin. But the damage had been done, leaving his reputation at zero and his nerves about to disintegrate.

"Any co-co-co-co-co-co?"

"Coffees on the boil," anticipated the cook, wearing the same dead-pan expression, oblivious to the sniggers circulating the room. Lieutenant James waved the interruption away, determined to overcome the problem. "Any co-co-co-co-co?"

"Cock-ups?" suggested a balding regular with the profile of a monkey and presumably the same level of intelligence.

The sweating officer glared at the caveman while we all waited, knowing he wouldn't give up.

"Any.... com..... plaints? Any complaints?" With increasing confidence he turned towards the cook. "Any complaints?"

"None at all."

"Jolly good." A look of relief spread across his undernourished face, bringing the eyebrows back in line. "In that case I'll have a chat with the men ... see how they're getting along."

He squinted around the room almost challenging someone to comment before moving warily between uncleaned tables - knowing he would have to engage someone in conversation. "What's that on your face, gunner?"

"Where, sir?"

"There! There!" He pointed repeatedly with the stick, hoping to reinstate his authority. "It looks very much like a smile."

"Can't be, sir." The hapless gunner transformed his face immediately. "I haven't got anything to smile about."

"Good, I'm glad to hear it."

Three cautious steps further, he paused again, neck turning from left to right barely touching his collar. "And are you men sh-sh-sh-sh-sh?"

Help came from three different directions, delivered with growing enthusiasm.

"Shagged out, sir?" - "Shit on, sir?" - "Shooting one another."

Lieutenant James used his stick to demand silence, wielding it like a conductor who had lost control of the orchestra. "No, no, no ... shaping up. Are you men shaping up?"

"Very well, thank you, sir." muttered a new recruit who hadn't seen the funny side of anything since his call up papers arrived.

"Fine, sir." reiterated another peacemaker with elevated ambitions.

'Jessie' James continued circling the tables, watching, waiting, hoping to select an easy target. "Name?"

An anxious looking lad shot to his feet, hoping not to panic as he tried to remember who he was. "Er...it's er... Walker, sir. Gunner Walker, A troop, number 257..."

"No need for all that nonsense. Just tell me what you think of the food."

"The...food, sir?"

"Yes, the food. What do you think of the food?"

Gunner Walker considered the implications of a wrong answer. "It's er...alright, sir."

The groans told Walker he had failed, unlike the lieutenant who silently congratulated himself. He had asked the right question to the right soldier and received the right answer.

Lieutenant James repositioned his stick and moved on, confidence growing as he headed for the door, pausing only to confirm his visit. "Well, at least there are no complaints."

"I have one, sir."

Every head turned in my direction, but only one had a frown.

"You have ...a complaint?" He made it sound like an incurable disease.

"Yes, sir. I'm afraid so."

They obviously hadn't covered this at the officer's training college. "No one has ever complained before."

"I find that hard to believe, sir. The food is a disgrace." I glanced towards the cook. "And the way it's served is no better."

The officer's stick went from one hand to the other as he struggled for a solution. "I hope you realise this is a very serious accusation ... very serious indeed."

"I'm glad you think so, sir. A lot of officers would ignore it. Would you prefer it in writing, sir? Or I could get a petition up. I'm sure most of the lads would sign it, they're always saying the food's crap."

Having regained his composure, the lieutenant now felt it slipping away as he faced what could be the beginnings of a rebellion; on top of which he now had an uncontrollable urge to empty his bladder. Logically he should exert his authority - that's what other officers would do, except they hadn't been brainwashed into believing they didn't have any. "You're new here aren't you, gunner?"

"Yes, sir. Tramp, sir."

The first sign of haemorrhoid pain convinced the lieutenant a more friendly approach, never before tried by officers of the Royal Artillery, could bring the matter to a speedy conclusion. "Ah, I thought so." He gave an unconvincing smile, squeezing his buttocks together in an attempt to ease the discomfort. "Still missing home cooking, I suppose?"

"Certainly am, sir."

"No one can cook like your mother, eh, gunner?"

"Well he certainly can't, sir. Then again there are only so many ways you can serve baked beans."

The first trickle ran down the inside of his leg as he fought to remain calm - the one quality that separated officers from other ranks. "I accept your views were made in all innocence so we'll say no more about it."

"But you asked if there were any complaints, sir."

Not for the first time, the army's newest commissioned officer suddenly doubted his ability to deal with difficult situations. He could sit all day experimenting with figures, making expenditure correspond with income, none of which upset his bodily functions. Now they threatened to overwhelm him as everyone waited expectantly for his response.

"Let me put it this way, gunner. If I meet someone in the street and ask how they are, I don't expect a m-m-m-m-m-m-m. Oh, blast and bugger. A m-m-m-m-m-m-m-m."

"Mouthful, sir?"

My suggestion went unheeded as he tried and tried again, finally succeeding at his fifth attempt. "Medical report ... I don't expect a medical report. Does that answer your question?"

"Well, not exactly, sir."

A rush of blood began to colour his face and, when he realised, the blush increased, along with a desire to disappear. "I'm not prepared to continue this ridiculous conversation. I've got more important things to do." Another trickle told him to hurry up and do them. "Take it up with Sergeant Jenkins."

"Do you think he'll be interested, sir?"

"How the bloody hell would I know." He headed for the door reminiscent of a German soldier performing a very slow goosestep.

"He deals with the problems around here."

"Is that because he causes them, sir?"

Lieutenant 'Jessie' James' urge to relieve his overflowing bladder and apply another tube of haemorrhoid cream, overcame any desire to defend Sergeant Jenkins or trade words with people of a lower class and intelligence. He galloped off, using the stick to hurry himself along.

His sudden departure left everyone speechless, apart from the cook, retrieving one and a half inches of cigarette from behind a 'NO SMOKING' sign. "I think he's in training for the Grand fucking National!"

We walked quietly back to the billet, even more aware of the power wielded by Sergeant Jenkins.

"The bastard has us by the short and curlies." Jock's optimism appeared to be going the same way as everyone else's. "He seems to control the whole sodding camp."

An air of gloom and despondency hung over the room as men of previous optimistic outlook sprawled about contemplating their future.

Timex continued walking aimlessly around, staring vacantly at his empty wrist, wondering why the replacement watch hadn't arrived. Jock puzzled over the state of his feet. Only Stan radiated any sign of life, whistling the theme from Bridge on the River Kwai. Thankfully a repeat performance came to an abrupt end as the door burst open.

"Stand by your beds!"

The sudden appearance of Lance Bombardier Dodds registered in our expressions as the shock of being caught relaxing turned the whole thing into a stampede.

"Stand fucking still!"

Only Timex failed to reach his bed, fearing the worst as he stood rigidly alongside an equally apprehensive Lancashire postman.

"What are you two doing?"

Stan managed to look suitably indignant, remembering a time when his mother caught him and a school pal comparing erections. "Nothing."

You just knew one of them would be in trouble as the NCO approached, treating the well polished floor with contempt as he spat twice in succession.

"Not really your day is it, Thomas, first complaining, and now caught in what can only be described as ... a compromising position."

Timex wanted to object, but either his nerve failed or he couldn't see the point, as Lance Bombardier Dodds moved to within licking distance of the Welshman. "People like you make me fucking sick!"

Timex paled visibly at the suggestion and the intimidation continued. "The army doesn't want queers so how did you get in?"

I knew he wouldn't defend himself. Arguments, however mild were not his forte, even debates left him at a loss for words. "He's no more queer than you are."

Dodds didn't expect me to interfere, faltering slightly at the realisation neither Hawkins nor the sergeant were on hand for support. "Who the hell asked your opinion, Tramp?"

"Just thought I'd straighten you out, Lance Bombardier."

"If anyone needs straightening out it's this bastard. He shouldn't be amongst normal people."

"We have no complaints about him, do we lads?"

Everyone gave their full support, none more vociferously than Jock, clearly incensed by this latest act of bullying.

"Why don't you get off the wee lad's back?"

The twin-pronged attack caused the NCO to bite his tongue, ruling out any immediate reprisals, other than verbal. "You fucking lot are getting too big for your boots. Just remember I can make your lives a bloody misery."

"He wished he could," whispered Jock to Leroy, but not quite soft enough.

"Oh, you don't think I can, eh! We'll soon see about that." He walked to the end of the billet, studying the blank walls for some form of divine inspiration. "Right, you're all volunteering to give blood." He allowed the news to sink in, giving no indication of when or where. "And I mean all of you. The people who extract the red stuff are civilians expecting a squad of highly trained soldiers who don't know the meaning of fear. Normally that would rule you lot out but they're short of donors, so don't pass out or breakdown. One more thing, you're volunteers, so look forward to it and smile. Make out you're enjoying yourselves. Is that clear?"

Hardly anyone replied, aware he was simply trying to regain his authority. Even the news of having to give blood failed to get the reaction he expected, leaving him very little choice other than to make a tactical exit. As a final face saver, he paused menacingly in front of a still traumatized Welshman.

"Report to me one hour from now."

Lance Bombardier Dodds' exit lacked the usual sighs of relief. In fact, his hasty departure preceded jeers and catcalls, although none loud enough for him to hear.

"I don't remember volunteering to give blood." Jock voiced everyone's concern. "Then again I didn't volunteer for the fucking army!"

"Neither did I … volunteer to give blood, I mean." Stan anxious not to give the wrong impression quickly re-established his position. "Not that it bothers me."

"It bothers me." Steve didn't look happy at all as recollections of being held down by a domineering father who couldn't understand his fear of needles came flooding back. "I passed out three times at the medical. When they informed us of the need for injections, watching others receive theirs, and then again when the doctor said, *roll your sleeves up.*"

Jock didn't appear too concerned with Steve's aversion to pain.

"I used to give blood most Saturday nights."

"You can't give blood that often."

"You can if some bastard thumps your nose."

Everyone smiled except Timex, knowing that his meeting with Dodds wasn't to discuss his promotional possibilities. "What do you think he'll do, Joe?"

"Oh, it's probably an evening with the potato peeler. You'll come back with blue fingers and a crick in your neck."

We both knew it wouldn't be anything so simple and for once I welcomed Stan's interruption.

"If I went to America I'd get paid for giving blood."

"I know, mate. But by the time you'd paid your fare..."

"I've never given blood."

Steve's confession hardly came as a surprise, neither did Stan's. "I haven't either … but I have thought about it."

"There's nothing to it, mate ... providing there are no complications." I prized Stan's fingers from my arm. "Calm down. It's very rare anything goes wrong. if it does, there's always a doctor standing by."

The fingers returned. "A doctor! What the hell's he there for?"

"Just a precaution, that's all."

"How much do they actually take?" Steve tried to sound matter of fact as he waited for something encouragement.

"Depends how much they need, mate ... but never more than a gallon."

The would-be lawyer wasn't fooled, unlike Stan who thought he was going to be sick.

"A bloody gallon? I don't think I've got that much."

Jock wasn't convinced. "Sounds a lot to me. I've got a gallon can back home."

"You don't have to supply your own container, mate. They provide the buckets."

"Bucket? They put it in a bucket?"

"Doesn't take long ... it comes out like a tap."

"So how do they know when to stop?"

"As soon as you pass out. That's why they make you lay down. I remember this one poor sod ... Christ, it was terrible."

Jock acknowledged my wink with a mumbled obscenity, while Steve retreated with a shake of the head. Only Stan remained concerned. "What happened?"

"One minute he was laying down quietly on the bed trying to look up some tart's skirt, the next trying desperately to stem the flow of blood from his arm."

"Where was the doctor?"

"In the next room giving the nurse one."

"The bastard!"

"Luckily a bloke on the next bed realised what was happening and fed the tube back into his mouth."

"Bloody hell!"

"Yeah, it saved his life, but by then he was addicted. The last I heard he was drinking ten pints of blood a day and eating six pounds of black pudding."

My ability to maintain a straight face had Stan baffled, but only for a matter of seconds. "Lying sod! You must think I was born yesterday."

Timex didn't return until almost midnight, tired and withdrawn, reluctant to discuss his last few hours, leaving us to draw our own conclusions.

Chapter 8

At 1400 hours under darkening skies and a strong westerly wind, oblivious to the regulations regarding litter as it swirled small clusters of red and brown leaves onto the parade ground, we were taken to meet Captain Fosdyke, officer in charge of personnel and confidante to the CO.

Advance knowledge supplied by previous intakes of national servicemen now classified as veterans, suggested he was an upper class twit, whose progress up the promotion ladder was assured, thanks to well-connected family members, including two colonels and a general who served with distinction during the evacuation of Dunkirk.

This was to be our belated welcoming speech and first words of advice, apart from those of a NAAFI cleaner with a smile extolling the advantages of having a low IQ and the ability to grin idiotically every time anyone approached. We appreciated the information, pointing out it hadn't got him far.

Fifteen minutes past the appointed time, we were ordered to stand by Bombardier Caddick, confusing the majority already on their feet who immediately sat down in an attempt to obey the command.

The shambolic manoeuvre received the captain's praise, surprising the relieved NCO, who had visions of being reduced to the ranks and spending his remaining eight month's service transferring fifty tons of coal ten yards to the right.

"Thank you, Bombardier. An excellent turnout. Well done."

"Will that be all, sir, or do you want me to stay and keep the fu... the men in order?"

Captain Fosdyke waved away the offer. "That won't be necessary, they look a thoroughly well-behaved squad to me."

Bombardier Caddick had his doubts, as he did about most things. Even a course on positive thinking failed when he couldn't decide whether to take the exam or not. "If you're sure, sir?"

"Of course I'm sure. They respect me and I er ... appreciate their difficulties. Now run along and leave me to get familiar with the men."

The Bombardier gave a crisp salute, in contrast to the officer's casual flick of the cap - which failed to impress both the bombardier and a rather lanky Geordie, whose brand new uniform failed to take account of anyone with exceptionally long arms. "He better not try and get fucking familiar with me."

The captain diplomatically failed to hear, positioning himself on the corner of a leather-topped desk, left leg swinging backwards and forwards as he surveyed the sea of blank faces. "Welcome to the Royal Artillery, gentlemen."

A friendly smile was met with open hostility, confirming the earlier impression we had very little to worry about for the next couple of hours.

"I can see you are all nervous. No need to be. This isn't a lecture, more a sort of meeting, a very informal sort of meeting." The smile remained. "Well not really a meeting - more of er ... a discussion, to discuss the formalities, but very informally."

"What's he rambling on about?" enquired a dimple-cheeked con-script with the nickname 'Ferret' whose two previous attempts to escape failed when the chain came off his bike.

"Those of you who wish to smoke may do so. We like everyone to feel at home."

The lad from Newcastle placed both feet on the table before extend-ing an arm as if demonstrating the inadequate sleeve length. "Alright if we have a nap, sir?"

The captain's leg missed a beat. "Officers make jokes, gunner. You merely laugh at them. Understood?"

"Yes, sir! Just tell us when you've made one."

This time the leg stopped completely as he considered the reply. When it eventually resumed swinging, we knew the Geordie had got away with it. The captain's second mistake, on top of the initial error in allowing Bombardier Caddick to leave. "I think at this stage a few introductions are in order. My name is Captain Fosdyke. DSO."

His intention to expand on the family's military achievements failed to get started as the big Geordie lad rose quickly to his feet, closely followed by three quarters of the room.

"Gunner Bent, GPO!"

"Taffy Williams, RSPCA!"

"Clive Roberts, master butcher!"

77

"Fred Harris, masturbator!"

"Silence! All of you." The earlier fixed smile had long since turned into a scowl, now directed at the half-a-dozen still standing, eager to announce their presence. "Sit down! Obviously discipline is not one of your strong points."

Captain Fosdyke thoughtfully stroked the thin line of dark hair along his top lip, as if deciding whether to shave it off or persevere in order to emulate pictures of his great-great grandfather who survived the charge of the Light Brigade during the Crimean War when his horse had a refusal at the first fence. Eventually he managed to drag his thoughts back to the present, aware of the growing restlessness permeating the room. "My job is to inform you about army life ... the prospects and the pitfalls. A task I've performed many times and yet one I still find extremely difficult."

"Just do your best, sir, we'll understand."

Captain Fosdyke glared long and hard at Stan before giving him the benefit of the doubt. "As I was saying, I'm here to prepare you for the daily routine of parades, inspections, and all the other disciplines that will turn you into soldiers. You will then be assessed in order to establish which particular branch of the artillery you will suit you best once you're out of training. We also encourage participation in some form of sport ... football, rugby, cricket." Captain Fosdyke wanted to include his favourite sport, but he wasn't sure they would understand the high degree of skill and fitness required for croquet. Lack of enthusiasm led him to believe something other than throwing or kicking a ball may spark their interest. "Does anyone have a hobby, however unusual?"

A teenager with galloping acne rose slowly to his feet. "I've got a lurcher, sir."

"If the MO confirms it, gunner, you will of course be excused."

The surrounding smiles were a clear indication he'd hit the right note with hobbies and this led to a ten-minute sermon on their merits during which he was oblivious to the small pockets of conversation that sprang up around the room.

"Any news from Wendy, mate?"

Timex limited his response to a disconsolate shake of the head - clearly reluctant to chat, particularly about Wendy, who he now assumed to be having it off with half the male population of Swansea.

Further attempts to converse ended when the Welshman turned away so I did the same, hoping someone else may feel more sociable. "How are you doing, mate?"

Steve's legal training prevented anything other than a long drawn out, carefully worded reply. "During the first week I regretted not accepting the chance of a commission ... better food, room of your own and not so much bullshit. But if these officers are anything to go by I'm glad I turned it down."

Steve continued to frown as he half listened to the captain boring the few remaining listeners with his interpretation of what constituted a hobby.

"Surely they can't all be like him, Joe."

"The ones we've come across so far appear to be."

He leaned over the table so I did likewise, anticipating another disparaging comment regarding the quality of Royal Artillery officers.

"I wrote to my father outlining a few of the problems we've come up against, especially those involving Timex."

"And?"

"He appeared to suggest we were exaggerating the situation ... said I never could stand up for myself. So much for parental concern."

The disappointment was evident so I tried not to make it worse. "Some fathers are like that. They just go about it the wrong way."

"Mine certainly did. His idea of swimming lessons consisted of throwing you in at the deep end and walking off. I couldn't even tell him I was being bullied at school or it would've been boxing gloves on while he knocked seven bells out of me. Then as a final humiliation, on my eighteenth birthday he entrusted the loss of my virginity to a local prostitute ... said it would make a man of me."

"And did it?"

"I still can't swim or stand up for myself and, in his eyes, I'm still not a man."

Steve's frank confession didn't make him less of a man in my eyes - in fact it required a great deal of guts to admit everything. Further revelations were terminated when Captain Fosdyke, suddenly aware he was talking mainly to himself, gave three hearty claps in an attempt to attract attention. "If anyone has something to say, perhaps we should all hear it." When no one took up the offer he assumed control, returning to his position on the desk, left leg resuming its metronome-like swing. "This is probably the first time many of you have lived away from home so it is bound to feel a little strange. I know from experience how difficult living with someone can be."

"I know exactly what you mean, sir." Gunner Wright had a reputation for saying the wrong thing, at the wrong time, to the wrong people. Having already upset two officers, we waited to see whether this would be number three. "My marriage didn't last either."

The remark turned the captain's normally pale features red with fury. "For your information, gunner, I've never been married."

"You do surprise me, sir."

"It don't fucking surprise me," mumbled Geordie Bent, acknowledging the sniggers as Captain Fosdyke rose to a height of six feet one inch. Unfortunately, his authority only went to three feet six.

"I was referring to the problems you'll encounter between yourselves, which I'm sure can be kept to a minimum with a little tolerance and understanding."

The surrounding expressions didn't quite mirror the captain's confidence.

"Today I want to talk about something traditionally British, in fact most of you will do it at least once a week. Can anyone tell me what it is?"

"Don't you know, sir?"

"Of course I know, you idiot." He felt confident dealing with Gunner Wright, wishing everyone else had the same simple-minded outlook. "I've done it enough times … still do occasionally."

"Is it wanking, sir?"

A mate ruffled what was left of Gunner Wright's hair. "He said once a week, not every bloody day."

Captain Fosdyke could get quite depressed at the way people continually took advantage: school chums who made him do things he didn't enjoy; work colleagues jealous of his financial standing; and now humble gunners with their sly smirks and mucky innuendoes. "That's not what I meant, why don't you listen?" He thought about other officers and the way they commanded immediate respect. He decided he would never come into that category. "I'm still waiting for someone to tell me what it is the British Army rely on."

"Is it ... the Americans, sir?"

Captain Fosdyke took consolation from the fact he could always control his temper - unlike the majority of officers who considered verbal abuse and, on occasions, physical violence to be an essential part of an officer's make-up. "I am in fact talking about guard duty ... a custom unrivalled by any other country in the world ... a custom perfected through years of training ... a custom..."

"Christ, he's off again."

The interruption produced nothing more than a slight delay in the rather muddled explanation. "Guard duty," Fosdyke continued, "is a very important part of army life.... very important." He tried without success to think why. "Therefore it's important to treat it with er...."

"Importance, sir?"

"Thank you, gunner, but I can manage. Now we must press on ... plenty more traditions to discuss."

"Aren't you going to explain a little more about guard duty, sir?"

Captain Fosdyke had inherited many of his mother's qualities, but very few of his father's, leaving him lacking in grit and determination but proficient in knitting and cookery. "The problem is we only have a limited amount of time." When no one accepted the excuse, mainly through lack of interest, his resolve began to crumble. "If we do it will have to be brief. I'm simply going to run through the relevant points ... hopefully without interruption."

His timid warning went unheeded as he positioned himself back on the desk, left leg resuming its sleep-inducing swing. "Let us assume you are on guard duty for the very first time." His voice dropped dramatically in an attempt to heighten the suspense. "Suddenly someone approaches from out of the darkness. Can anyone tell me the first course of action?"

"Piss off!" mumbled long armed Geordie Bent, earning himself nothing more than a mild frown.

"Shoot the bastard." suggested another who wasn't quite so lucky.

"What's your name, gunner?"

"Miller."

"Miller, what?"

"Miller ... sir."

A small notebook containing a blue 2H pencil, previously used to remove earwax appeared from a breast pocket.

"You're on a charge, Miller."

"What for, sir?"

Unsure of the procedure, he chose to ignore the question, reminding himself to have a word with Major Hill, recognised authority on army punishment. "The idea of being on guard duty is to stop anyone entering who could be a danger to the whole camp."

"So we don't let the cooks in, sir?"

The notebook came into view for the second time. "Name?" "Tramp, sir."

"As I was saying, guard duty is a very responsible job, therefore you must challenge anyone who approaches."

"What at, sir?"

Another name entered the book, scribbled alongside the address of a mail order company who specialised in ladies lingerie. No one under the rank of lieutenant could possibly understand the need for wearing women's knickers, or the excitement of displaying a white, lacy bra to a similarly clad officer. "Anyone else interrupting will receive the same treatment. I don't care if we're here all day."

"You said we only had a limited amount of time, sir."

"I don't care what I said earlier."

"So all of this has been a waste of time, sir?"

Captain Fosdyke pushed aside all thoughts of parading in skimpy outfits, determined to gain the upper hand. "I don't think you're listening, gunner, or perhaps you have a hearing problem."

"Pardon, sir?"

"I said do you have a problem with your ears?"

The lad with galloping acne, and a love of lurchers, gave a good indication why he failed the eleven plus and just about every other exam he'd ever taken. "No, not really, sir. I've always had a big arse."

Captain Fosdyke waited for the giggles to subside before entering name number four - the rather laboured procedure giving him time to try and combat the growing feeling of despair.

His attempt at governing by silence - as practised successfully by the artillery's only stone deaf officer - failed to stop the yawns spreading and in no time at all most of the lads had their mouths, with the exception of Leroy, chasing a spider around the table with two out-stretched fingers.

"Where do they get these officers from, Joe? They don't appear to have a clue."

"I agree. Can you imagine him standing up to Sergeant Jenkins?"

"I still think we should tell him what's going on, if only for Gerry's sake."

We became conscious of others listening to the conversation, including the captain, acutely aware his *friendly approach* treatment hadn't really worked.

"When you've finished perhaps we can continue, or would you prefer to take over the class?"

He directed the question at Leroy, in his mind the easier target, but I intervened on his behalf. "No, sir ... you carry on."

"Well thank you. It's nice to know I have your permission to continue. Now if you have nothing better to do perhaps we can try again." The hint of sarcasm and open notebook deterred anyone from testing what little patience he had left. "If someone approaches whilst you are on guard, ask if they are friend or foe? If they reply friend and you fail to recognise them ask for some means of identification."

Leroy leant back in his chair, long legs stretching across the aisle. "What happens if the answer is foe, sir?"

"I thought that would be obvious even to a nig nog. You don't let them in! You do know what foe is?"

"Do dat come after tree, sir?"

Leroy's name went into the book before I could distract Captain Fosdyke with the kind of question guaranteed to test his patience. "What if they are the enemy claiming to be friends, sir?"

"It would be totally unethical for anyone to try and gain advantage in such a manner. Totally unethical."

"I didn't think there were any ethics in war, sir."

"Even the enemy has a code of honour, gunner, and there is such a thing as the Geneva Convention." He dismissed further attempts to prolong the conversation with a defiant shake of the head. "I don't think these type of questions serve any relevant purpose."

"You did say to ask if we didn't know, sir." I adopted a hurt expression, previously used in a failed attempt to make Judy feel guilty after accusing me of infidelity. "In future I'll keep my mouth shut."

"So will I."

"And me."

Support came thick and fast from every direction, reducing the captain to little more than a spectator.

"I shan't come again."

"I feel like leaving right now. Balls to the lecture."

The captain's record of never having lost his temper hung in the balance, but not for long as his voice began to rise, reaching the level formerly demanded by a bullying drill sergeant in order to attack a straw dummy with fixed bayonet. "Silence! I'm not putting up with this from a bunch of no-*fucking*-hopers. Who the bloody hell do you think you're talking to?" A trembling finger pointed towards the only person still on his feet. "And you, fucking sit down, nobody's going anywhere until I say so. Is that clear?"

He repeated the question in a voice somewhere between tenor and alto. "I said is that clear?"

The mumbled replies and shocked faces slowly reduced the officer's level of anger. "Count yourselves lucky you're not dealing with the CO otherwise you'd all be in the guardroom by now."

We watched and listened, unimpressed as he explained with stern facial expressions combined with exaggerated hand gestures, the type of punishment we could expect if our disgraceful behaviour continued.

Having re-established superiority, at least in his mind, the beleaguered officer realised he still had to finish explaining the basic procedure for guard duty. "Assuming we are faced with a potentially dangerous situation … for example, a complete stranger trying to gain access … you must hold them at bay with your rifle."

"Is it loaded, sir?"

"For safety reasons we are only allowed live ammunition in emergencies."

"How do we kill people then, sir?"

Captain Fosdyke stared long and hard, eventually deciding it was the kind of question you could expect from the lower classes and therefore of no consequence. "As I was saying, we are not allowed to issue ammunition. However, should the occasion arise you are to proceed as follows."

He cleared his throat and I knew it would be a long, boring explanation - so did the others.

"Oh, Christ! Here we go again."

"What a load of balls."

"I can't take much more of this."

"Make absolutely sure it is the enemy, not one of the officers returning from a fancy dress party."

The expected smiles never materialised, squashing his grin before it could set. "In a firm voice order your foe to remain perfectly still, with their hands where you can see them. This is very important because they could have a concealed weapon in their trousers, and the minute your back's turned they could whip it out and you'd be..."

"Buggered, sir."

"Exactly." Captain Fosdyke took full credit for the giggles. "Assuming the enemy are under control you are now in a position to call the guard sergeant who, in turn, reports to the duty officer, requesting a note for the issue of one bullet. The note is then taken to the QM, who will exchange it for one live bullet, with instructions to reload. You can now confront your enemy, remembering to point the rifle upwards, not directly at anyone in case it goes off."

As excitement mounted, at least for the captain, everyone else having lost interest, he continued the build-up to a nail-biting climax. "With the enemy under control, you then repeat the original order in two different languages ... thereby complying with the rules laid down by the Geneva Convention."

"I can't speak two languages, sir."

This frank admission to a limited education had the support of anyone still awake, much to the officer's surprise.

"You don't have to be fluent, you're not going to carry on an hour long conversation."

"It's a load of bollocks if you ask me."

Captain Fosdyke considered the size of Bomber Harris and turned away. "Can anyone speak a second language?"

"Does sign language count, sir?"

"It does if your prisoner's fucking deaf." replied Bomber, displaying a full set of teeth.

"Thank you, Gunner Harris, but we can do without those kind of comments." Addressing Ferret with something approaching genuine surprise. "So you can do sign language."

Ferret hurriedly concealed his latest plan of escape before considering the consequences of lying. "Er... no, sir."

Fosdyke began to have second thoughts about his career - even his sanity came into question as he looked around trying to make sense of it all. Having been promised travel and adventure, he now found himself stagnating in a place aptly named, surrounded by adults with a mental age of ten.

"How many of you have been abroad?"

A few half-hearted nods encouraged him to continue. "And didn't you pick anything up?"

"I picked up a bit of Spanish, sir." Bomber Harris's smirk confirmed he was about to take advantage of the officer's unfortunate choice of words. "She had long dark hair, smouldering eyes and a pair of tits you..."

"That's enough, gunner. I'm sure nobody wants to hear about your sordid little affairs."

"I do, sir."

"And me."

Having already gone through a variety of emotions, Fosdyke no longer had the energy or inclination to hand out further reprimands, even his voice lacked the confidence of earlier. "I really don't see the point in carrying on."

"Don't let it get you down, sir." Stan's well intentioned sympathy hardly endeared himself to the captain. "We've all felt suicidal at one time or another, haven't we lads?"

"Still fucking do." exclaimed the long-armed Geordie, examining the contents of his nose.

"I am not suicidal, you brainless cretin, although I may be if I remain here much longer." The captain, preparing himself for a quick exit, still had one last message to deliver. "As officer in charge of personnel, I'm responsible for the welfare of national servicemen, both in and out of camp. Any problems, come and see me ... preferably at the onset. Don't wait for things to escalate. If you're unhappy with something, tell me about it. No point in writing to your mother."

Before he could conclude, Timex stood up, his sullen expression matched only by that of the captain. "We're in 'S' squad, sir. Sergeant Jenkins outfit."

"Well, thank you for that information, gunner. Now if there's nothing else."

When the Welshman sat down again, I knew his resolve had evaporated. "I think what Gunner Thomas is trying to say is that Sergeant Jenkins and his henchmen are nothing more than bullying, sadistic bastards, sir." If the information came as a shock, he certainly didn't show it.

"I know the sergeant can be a little ... forceful at times."

"Is that what you call it, sir?"

"Perhaps you're over-reacting, gunner."

"I don't think so, sir."

"Have you any evidence of this so-called ... bullying?"

"I think the lads would confirm the sort of treatment we've had to put up with," - I refrained from commenting on specific incidents - "nn more than one occasion, sir."

"So it's your word against that of senior NCOs."

I didn't answer, well aware of his next line of defence.

"You'll require far more evidence if you expect the matter to be investigated." Captain Fosdyke clearly didn't have the stomach for either arguing or retaliation, sighing with relief as he hurried towards the door.

"Before you leave, sir," Gunner Riley had a complex about his lack of inches and therefore remained seated, "could you explain the rules of the Geneva Convention?"

The disillusioned officer continued his march to freedom and sanity. "Balls to the Geneva Convention."

Chapter 9

To improve our survival skills, we had to construct a raft, capable of carrying men and equipment over rivers and lakes, using a selection of fallen trees, rope and ingenuity.

We set about the task with unbridled enthusiasm, cheering loudly as the raft began its descent down a muddy bank to await the arrival of captain and crew. The launch surpassed expectations, remaining afloat for at least twenty seconds before slowly submerging. Cries of 'Abandon Ship' failed to remove a newly appointed Welsh lance bombardier whose boat building skills consisted of tying lengths of wood together with rope while reciting 'A boy stood on the burning deck.' Fearing a rapid return to the ranks, combined with a dislike of water, he refused to leave his post - holding a tense salute as he sang the first verse from 'Land of my Fathers'. His intention to include the chorus, followed by a repeat in Welsh, came to an abrupt end as the craft hit the bottom, stranding him in three feet of water.

The only casualty occurred when a gunner, watching horrified from the bank, embarked on a rescue mission with a perfectly executed swallow dive. It took three of us to pull his head out of the mud and another six to retrieve his cap.

We returned to the billet wet, tired and hungry, in desperate need of female company. At least I was in desperate need; the others were mostly homesick. As usual Timex fetched out pen and paper to record the day's events, including a sketch of the raft and details of our lucky escape.

Without the postmark, Wendy might think we were on active service in a remote part of the world - that's if she ever bothered to read the letters.

Jock's daily strip show now incorporated a personal inspection, after complaining of a burning sensation when urinating. "Perhaps I'd better show it to the MO."

"Why not? You've shown it to everyone else."

Steve declined an invitation for a closer investigation, turning his back in disgust. "I wish he wouldn't keep messing with himself - it's unhygienic."

Leroy concentrated his energy, polishing a right boot to the same high standard as the left, holding the finished article at arms length. "Do you know, I think I could win a prize with this."

"So could I," leered the Scotsman, leaping naked onto Leroy's bed, displaying the only part of his anatomy to disperse feelings of inadequacy. "Don't you think, pal?"

"Oh, for Christ's sake!" moaned the black fireman. "Do we have to put up with this every night?"

Stan's fascination with the cinema was, if anything, more boring then Jock's addiction to indecent exposure as he bombarded us with facts and figures in between reviewing the latest Hollywood epic.

"The Americans have just released Ben-Hur into this country."

"That's all we need," sneered Jock, whose last visit to a cinema produced three tons of lead flashing. "More ex-convicts."

"No, he's not a convict. He drives a chariot."

"I don't give a monkey's what he drives. We don't want the buggers over here. And the names Chevrolet not Chariot."

Although I occasionally enjoyed a bit of cabaret, I didn't particularly want to hear it every evening, or listen to Timex's pathetic whining about having written more than thirty letters without response. Almost in desperation I telephoned the Royal Oak pub, hoping the barmaid's kindness included counselling soldiers who were harbouring thoughts of violence towards their room-mates. Much to my surprise, Julie remembered our first meeting and had no hesitation in suggesting I join her for a drink at around eight thirty.

Twenty minutes before the agreed time, while others were strolling aimlessly about the camp in groups of three or four, sharing their secrets for pressing uniforms or getting the best out of boot polish, I approached the uninspiring guard, small, white fingers wrapped around a rifle looking far more menacing than he ever could. A weak, almost apologetic smile brightened his pale features and you knew instantly he was national service. Regulars either spat or cursed to show they were men of the world. He began to march up and down, the exaggerated movement of his arms lifting the bony shoulders almost to ear level. I passed a friendly comment but he became suspicious, unsure of whether a reply might put the whole camp at risk. Maybe he was unsure about everything - his life, sex, which sock to put on.

The evening air, cool and damp as you would expect for late October, now had a smell of frost which tickled your nose with every breath. I strode past well-lit shops - their usually drab windows were now a colourful display of rockets, Catherine wheels and mighty atoms, strong enough to blow someone's fingers off.

It seemed only yesterday we were dropping them through letterboxes and helping bonfire organizers by setting them alight a day early. Mr Pugh, ex-war hero whose cat still hadn't come back down the chimney, came after us with a loaded rifle threatening to annihilate everyone under the age of fifteen. A jumping jack exploded at the same time. Three of us had the presence of mind to collapse, writhing in agony, earning a bravery award, unlike Mr Pugh, who received a prison sentence for possessing illegal weapons and ill-treating the cat.

With time to spare, I entered the Royal Oak. A roaring coal fire reminded me of home. The few early evening drinkers, swapping stories of much vaunted sexual accomplishments, would continue their lies when they arrived home, complaining of working late and being exploited by a boss who didn't appreciate their input. If the excuses were plausible, the possibility of a much-needed shag lay ahead to relieve the frustrations of spending eight hours lusting after a well-developed office junior who threatened to report the next person who commented on the size of her tits.

I walked over to my date. "Sorry I'm late." Julie looked up at me. She was even more attractive than I remembered, or perhaps the make-up and different hairstyle made her appear more sophisticated.

"That's okay, I've only just arrived myself."

"I'm not usually late."

"That's okay."

"I just had to pop back and change. I'm sure you wouldn't want me smelling of beer and smoke."

The way I felt, she could tread in dog shit and still be desirable. "It's okay, honestly."

She undid a red, fur-trimmed coat, fumbling with the solitary button as if unsure whether to remove it. "How's your friend, the one with the er...?"

"Oh, he's okay."

We looked in different directions, Julie unconcerned as customers smiled at her and glared at me.

"How are you enjoying army life?"

"It's er...." I resisted using okay in case she assumed I had a very limited vocabulary. "It's alright." For some reason I appeared incapable of putting a sentence together. I turned my attention to a stuffed owl staring down from a glass-fronted case. He didn't know what he was doing here either.

Sensing my unease, she placed a warm hand on mine. "We could always go elsewhere - if you prefer."

"Yes, if you don't mind."

"Make a nice change. After all, I'm stuck behind the bar nearly every night of the week." The smile broadened as she leaned closer and I could see the mischief in her eyes. "Give them all something to talk about."

Outside, Julie fastened her coat, pulling the collar high as a gust of wind swept strands of hair across her face. The use of lacquer, as recommended by Miss Cooper, had long since been forgotten, along with the correct use of hands and ability to perfect the *little girl lost* expression. Miss Cooper's School for young Gals hardly applied to a barmaid working in Gravesend.

I considered removing the strands so I could feel feel the softness of her skin with the back of my hands but the distance between us remained as we turned into the High Street.

Within the space of ten minutes I discovered Julie Townsend disliked three things - bad time keeping, untidiness and infidelity. The fact that I excelled at all three didn't bode well for a lasting relationship.

"I did tell my father I wouldn't be late." She sensed my disappointment. "Why don't you come and meet him, I'm sure you have a lot in common."

The invitation caught me by surprise. Few of my former girlfriends had been so hospitable, even after half-a-dozen dates. The ones who were usually lived to regret it, none more so than Shirley Wood, whose father Billy just happened to be a workmate. But at least it stopped his daily taunt - 'Which little scrubber did you get your leg over last night, Joe?'

From the High Street, we turned left, followed by two rights, another left and a final right, leading us into a small cul-de-sac surrounding a single oak tree - a sad reminder of when such giants where in abundance.

"That's my house." Julie pointed towards a neat semi-detached, its recently creosoted window box already prepared for a colourful Spring. "We've been here five years."

Dead oak leaves scuttled to meet us, nestling around our feet before a gust of wind swept them in to the air. A handful followed us into the porch where they would remain until someone else arrived. We entered the house. A dark brown carpet made a welcome change from the bare linoleum back at camp. Even the light appeared brighter, while the smell reminded me of home - a mixture of freshly cooked food and coal fires.

She gave me a nudge. "Joe, this is my father."

You could almost feel the pride in her voice as I stepped forward, nodding slightly as I extended my hand. "Pleased to meet you, sir."

The touch of reverence raised one eyebrow before his craggy features formed into a rather lopsided smile, reminiscent of our old science teacher who had suffered a stroke. Others blamed an unfortunate experiment and promptly nicknamed him Frankenstein. "Glad to meet you, young fellow."

He had a firm handshake and a voice of authority, backed up by a physique that wouldn't be out of place in a rugby scrum. I certainly couldn't imagine him backing down.

"We don't get many visitors, do we, love?"

His daughter agreed and I wondered why. Unless he was over-protective? Fathers could be that way inclined when left to bring up a child.

The majority of attractive females in Wolverhampton were often swept off their feet before they left school, either by a sugar daddy or a fifteen stone factory worker who put her on a par with his whippet.

A large oak sideboard complete with wedding photos and the standard fruit bowl dominated one side of the living room. Opposite, a cumbersome fireplace, piled high with lifeless coal.

"Dad, you've put too much on." She leaned closer, unable to see a single flame - just clouds of smoke billowing up the chimney. "I told you to leave it alone."

He shrugged a pair of hefty shoulders, obviously used to the occasional scolding. "See what I have to put up with? Just like her mother."

That figured because she certainly didn't resemble her father, apart from the same twinkling eyes. I put his age around fifty, although the greying hair and glasses probably made him look older - not to mention the baggy trousers and sweater, a real granddad's outfit. "Julie says you've lived here five years."

"That's right, we moved here when her mother died." For long, silent moments the twinkle left his eye and I wondered what he missed most - the company, sex, home cooking or just someone to care about. I always wanted to ask Ma the same question but maybe it was a little too personal.

Silence didn't appear to bother father or daughter, clearly used to quiet evenings.

"I believe you've travelled extensively." I omitted the word, sir, in case it sounded patronising.

"Not exactly, but I've been ...we've been around quite a bit. Comes with the job."

"Dad served twenty five years in the army."

I glanced towards Julie, puzzling why she had never mentioned it before. "So what regiment were you with?" I felt like an old soldier about to exchange army stories, except mine would be limited to Jock's obsession with his reproductive organs.

"Same as you, young fellow, Royal Artillery."

"I didn't realise. So you know all about this camp."

The atmosphere between us stiffened, along with his expression, warning me against further questions.

"I've been out of the army ... three, nearly four years. Times change, people come and go."

"But you must've come across Sergeant Jenkins?"

His brief glance towards Julie spoke volumes - most of them asking why the hell did she bring me back. "We crossed swords occasionally. Are you in his squad?"

"Unfortunately, yes."

Having stated my position, I waited for a reaction, acutely aware he could be a bigger bastard than Jenkins.

"At least you won't be with him long."

"Why, is he retiring?"

His brief shake of the head dismissed any hope in that direction. "He wouldn't survive in civvy street."

"You're dead right he wouldn't." My next comment could make this a short-lived visit, scuppering any chance of gaining credibility with his daughter. "There must be thousands of national servicemen planning his downfall. I wonder how brave he is without the army to support him."

"Don't underestimate the man ... he's as tough as old boots"

"That doesn't give him the right to treat people the way he does. We're not at war now. He's already responsible for half-a-dozen suicides." The slight exaggeration went unchallenged. "There'll be another one soon unless something's done about him."

"I admit his methods are a little ... unorthodox, but I'm afraid I can't help you, Joe."

I wanted to scream, this was a little more than 'unorthodox', but that would really be pushing my luck. "Even the officers appear reluctant to do anything, and they must know what's going on. We even considered approaching the CO."

My unwavering stare eventually dragged out a response.

"I'm afraid you won't achieve much there. Jenkins and the CO go back a long way, and therein lies the problem. They were together all through the war. The CO was only a captain then but his so-called bravery soon gained him promotion and the Distinguished Service Medal for exceptional gallantry."

"For doing what?"

"You would need to ask Sergeant Jenkins. He was the only one with him at the time."

I gained the distinct impression things were not hunky-dory between the two men. Perhaps time to express a few opinions.

"It's almost as though Jenkins has some sort of a hold over the CO." The directness of my question caught him by surprise, leaving me in no doubt the assumptions were proving correct.

"My advice to you, young fellow, is to keep out of his way ... and that goes for the rest of your mates. Don't think his actions go unnoticed. The army's not completely run by fools even if this camp is."

Julie, sensing her father's growing irritation, stepped forward, hands on hips as she prepared to lay down the law. "Can we please change the subject?" Turning to her father. "I didn't bring Joe back to talk about the army. He has enough of that at camp." Before he could object she swung in my direction. "Dad's no longer in the artillery, so no more questions."

Before the silence became uncomfortable, she moved, or rather glided, gracefully towards the door. "Now who's for coffee?"

I nodded sulkily, unlike Mr. Townsend who screwed his nose up as though coffee was a dirty word.

"What do you prefer, young fellow, beer or coffee?"

With the atmosphere suddenly relaxed, I leant back, hands clasped behind my neck while I considered the options. "I think ... beer, please"

Julie's face showed she didn't approve. "Dad brews his own and it's very strong. He's used to it ... you're not."

My drinking prowess had never been in any doubt, other than a slight hiccup at a football presentation when a combination of beer and champagne sent me sliding under the table, alongside the goalkeeper and a half-naked waitress who only wanted his autograph. "Stop worrying - I've been drinking since I was twelve."

She left the room, unimpressed as her father returned carrying bottles and two pint glasses.

We emptied the first in relative silence, apart from a satisfying nod at the smooth taste. Previous offerings of home brew were either used to kill slugs or get rid of unwanted guests. Our tongues loosened midway through the second and by bottle number three we were chatting like old buddies - although we avoided any mention of earlier matters until bottle number six was empty.

"That Jenkins is a real bastard, Joe. Should have been kicked out years ago."

"Then why wasn't he?"

Ex-Sergeant Bill Townsend had palpitations, and only two things gave him that. The first was nightmares, occasions when he would wake up sweating as the horrors of war came flooding back. The other was – any mention of Jenkins. "The only person who can sanction that is the CO but instead of reading the riot act he continues to defend him. Jenkins gets a hundred percent support from the CO, even senior officers know better then to mess with him." He reached for the seventh bottle. "Now let's forget about Jenkins, he's not worth it."

Julie's was still scowling, appearing even sterner as she sat beside me. "You're drinking far too much ... don't forget you're not used to it."

If my calculations were correct, seven bottles equated to seven pints, divided by two leaves three and a half - less than I drank on a normal Sunday lunchtime.

"Stop worrying. Another pint and he'll be ready for bed." I reached for her hand, succeeding at the third attempt. "Then you ... and I ... can get to know one other ... one other ... nuther ... one anuner."

The hand pulled away. "See what I mean. You've had too much already."

Bottle number eight made Bill Townsend - Willy as I now began to call him - even more talkative. By the ninth, I realised just how funny he was - unlike his daughter, whose frown grew deeper and ever more threatening. "You're beginning to slur your words."

I squeezed the front of her thigh before she could move away. "Leave your dad alone, he's enjoying himself."

"I don't mean him," she hissed, putting even greater distance between us.

Bottle number ten left me with a permanent grin and a need to break wind. "Ooooooooops, I didn't know you had a dog."

Julie's look of disgust wasn't matched by her father's smile. He obviously had no idea what I intended to do with his daughter - come to think of it, neither did I.

Our respective positions at each end of the settee hardly made for whispered comments without leaning to the side.

"I think your dad's ... pissed." With extreme difficulty I managed to regain my upright posture at the expense of another fart. "Sounds like the dog's back again."

Julie was used to stupid comments and lecherous stares - it came with the job - but she hadn't expected either from me, hurriedly tugging the skirt over her shapely knees. "We haven't got a dog."

"In that case it must be one of us. Will the guilty cultrip ... cultriple ... culprik, pleash shtand up." When no one moved I eventually succeeded in standing upright, condemning myself with an unsteady finger directed somewhere between my nose and navel. "It's me, I know it's hard to believe...but it is. I'm the dirty bugger." An overwhelming urge to relieve myself failed to go unnoticed, or perhaps I gave the game away by repeatedly holding my testicles.

"The toilet's in the hall." She pointed towards a door, reminding me of a Victorian father dismissing his pregnant daughter. "And then I think you should leave - or someone's going to be ill."

I lurched forward, finger pressed hard against my lips. "Shhhhhhh - I know what you mean. He's drinking far too much. You wait until he tries to shtand."

Halfway through emptying my bladder, I remembered to lift the toilet seat, returning to the living room just in time to bid her father goodnight. "Did you see that? He couldn't even walk sshhtraight. I bet he's rough in the morning."

She sat down in disgust and I knew exactly how she felt - parents can be a real let down at times.

I joined her on the settee but she soon moved away, making an insipid face as the skirt received another tugging.

"I hope you're not going to be ill."

"Why, is it your turn?"

She ignored my giggles, emitting a long, deep, wearisome sigh. "You look awful."

"Thash funny...so do I."

"For the life of me I can't understand anyone drinking all that beer when they know it's going to make them ill."

My smile turned into a frown. "Neither can I."

"Grown men making complete fools of themselves."

"I think you're being a bit hard on your old man. He didn't look that bad to me."

She rose quickly, the way you do when there's nothing more to say. "I think you should be going, Joe. It's getting late."

I studied my watch with considerable curiosity, unable to believe the numbers had somehow been tampered with. "You're right." I made a clumsy attempt at a kiss but she turned her head.

"Should I ring for a taxi, Joe?"

"Why, are you going out?" Even my one-liners were letting me down - maybe it was time to go.

"I'm sorry, Joe … I shouldn't have brought you back here."

I raised an arm anticipating the rest. "I quite understand … no need to explain. You win some, you lose some."

Before I could move away two warm hands settled on my chest. "No, what I mean is … we should never have got you into this condition. I'm angry with my father who should know better. Maybe we can do it again another time."

"Well, if you think your dad's up to it."

This time she smiled while I was trying to be serious. I swear I'll never understand women!

"No, Joe. Just you and me."

I nodded, unable to believe she may want to see me again. Or perhaps it was simply a way of getting me out of the house. The feel of my lips on her cheek, the smell of her hair, not to mention the thought of those knees and what lay beyond, awoke a need, dulled by pint after pint of Willy's home brew. I did consider going back to give her one in the hall but I wasn't sure the need had reached below my waist and I didn't want to disappoint her for a second time.

The camp, situated on the outskirts of town, showed no visible signs of life, neither did the guard, fighting a losing battle against boredom as I crept up to the locked gates.

"Boo!"

His reaction surprised me, so did the rifle pointing at my stomach. "Who the fuck are you?"

I gave my rank, name and number - parrot fashion. I considered a salute to liven up the occasion but his face didn't encourage it.

"You're fucking national service." He made it sound like I was from a leper colony. Then again Fred Harris, shitty jobs expert, unmarried, unloved, unwelcome and unprompted after fifteen years, never was big on subtlety. "Fucking crap!"

"I bet you're a regular."

A look of suspicion hung over the demented features as he searched his vocabulary for a suitable reply. "So fucking what?" The rifle moved higher. "I could blow your fucking head off!"

"Not with that. It hasn't been fired in thirty years."

"Where's your fucking pass?"

"I've ... lost it."

"Then you can't fucking come in."

Stamping my feet up and down had two benefits. It improved circulation, thus combating the cold, and it temporarily delayed the desire to expel at least two pints of home brew. "Look, mate. I can't stand here all night."

"Why not? I've fucking got to."

"I have to be up early in the morning." I glanced at my watch, now able to get it in focus. "This morning, and I would like to get a few hours sleep."

"Don't talk to me about sleep. I've been on guard duty for three fucking nights." He leaned closer. "You've been fucking drinking."

I began to feel like a hardened criminal. "Don't tell me you never touch the stuff."

"I don't get the chance, I'm always on fucking guard."

"What the hell's going on out there?" From out of the shadows stepped Lance Bombardier Dodds, the initial show of anger subsiding as he approached. "Well, well, well, look who we have here ... Gunner bloody Tramp."

"Hello, Rose ... fancy seeing you here. We must stop meeting like this."

"I see you're still full of shit." He discharged the contents of his throat into the netting. "We'll soon knock that out of you."

"What do you want me to do with him, Charlie?"

"Unlock the gates and let him in."

The guard's protests were quickly dismissed. "Just do as you're told, Fred. You've been warned enough times about interfering in army matters."

"Then fuck you and the fucking army. You're all a bunch of fuck-ing...fuckers."

His anger didn't prevent the gates being opened, much to Dodds' relief. Reprimanding Gunner Fred Harris had a certain stigma to it, similar to bullying a spastic or bollocking the deaf. Anyone who could get away with telling the CO to fuck off, deserved a little credit.

"Stay on guard. Fred, don't let any bugger in for the next twenty minutes." Lance Bombardier Dodds fastened his battledress before turning in my direction. "Follow me."

I hesitated, watching the spittle stretch lower and lower as it clung to the netting. That's what I should be doing, clinging on instead of walking into a trap but for some reason my legs wouldn't co-operate. Or perhaps it no longer mattered.

We entered the guardroom in silence, three empty camp beds show-ing signs of recent use. The smell of unrecognisable food mixed with sweat and cigarettes wafted across the room as a door slammed behind, sealing the only means of escape. Four burly soldiers in various states of undress surrounded the lance bombardier as he whispered instruc-tions; brief glances confirmed their interest in my presence. One with a towel draped over his shoulders tossed it aside; another emptied the contents of an enamel mug before pulling on a pair of size twelve boots. The whole thing had a feeling of deja vu as I watched and waited -

anticipating the worst.

As the seconds ticked by, my hopes began to rise. No one had actually threatened or even approached me; in fact, I could be the invisible man. Lulled into a false sense of security I started to relax, unaware of a fifth soldier coming up from behind. A long handled club sliced through the air, burying itself deep into my midriff. Normally I would attempt some form of protection, but I simply stood there, offering no resistance as the blows increased. Odds of five to one did tend to make things a little one-sided - but that was no excuse. John Wayne always came through it without getting his cap knocked off.

I wanted to escape, not just the blows, but the whole bloody scenario. How I longed to be back home, no worries, no pain, waited on hand and foot instead of being bent first one way and then the other. I resembled a tree, clinging to life while the lumberjack swung away, burying his axe deeper and deeper.

I remembered grinning, but not for long as I sank slowly to the floor, praying for the nightmare to end. But they wouldn't co-operate, using fists and feet to every part of the body - only my face remained unmarked as it lay motionless against the dusty floorboards. Finally it stopped, and suddenly they were dragging my aching body across the room, panting and cursing as they hauled me down three head-jolting steps, on to soft spongy grass. The stuffy atmosphere was replaced by a welcoming breeze.

I remained conscious in a strange sort of suspended paralysis, only my eyes able to move as they watched the stars twinkle and fade. I imagined them finding me in the daylight, Stan, Jock, Steve, Leroy and Timex, standing unsmiling above me: no tears, no compassion.

"Shouldn't we close his eyes? They always do in the movies."

"No point, he can't see anything."

"In that case can I have his boots? They're better than mine."

"Can I have his belt? Shame to bury it."

"What about the uniform? Joe won't need it where he's going."

Tears began trickling down my face, disappearing into the damp grass. So this was it. Bon voyage, finito, farewell, adieu, the end of the line. I wanted to say a few last goodbyes - Ma, Christine, Susannah, Judy. Even Julie deserved a consideration - but where were they all? No one to hold my hand or kiss the cold, clammy cheeks; not even a priest to send me on my final journey. I began to hum *Abide With Me*, a real tear-jerker at the best of times - a poignant reminder of our mortality.

I heard someone approaching, perhaps an angel sent to show me the way. In ten minutes I could be wearing a shroud - walking amongst the clouds playing a harp. The footsteps stopped, followed by the unmistakable sound of a zip. Was I simply to be placed in a bag and thrown unceremoniously onto a tip?

The sound and feel of cascading fluid failed to register until my eyes eventually opened to the ultimate humiliation. "You dirty bastard!" I yelled, struggling to shield myself as the flow trickled into silence. But my assailant merely laughed, reversing the zip as he walked away whistling *Singing in the Rain*.

With great difficulty I managed to stand, in no position to do anything but curse as the back of Lance Bombardier Dodds disappeared into the well-lit guardroom. Even at twenty yards I could here the laughter as they congratulated themselves on a job well done. For long shivering moments, I debated my position; even considered the possibility of launching a counter-attack, but revenge would have to wait. Other things were far more pressing, particularly on my bladder. On top of which, I didn't smell too good.

Chapter 10

The clanging of locker doors and mumble of voices anxious not to be caught unprepared, were a stark reminder of my primitive conditions - dragging me from a much needed sleep before I could ravish Lorna Brown, every boy's fantasy at senior school. Once again, Reveille had saved her reputation at the expense of mine.

Fourteen year old Lorna, described as a disruptive influence, could attract more attention than the teachers simply by inhaling or crossing her shapely legs. She had the eyes of a seductress and a bigger bust than any one of her age, using them both to good effect to further her career at the expense of other people's.

No-one, it seemed, could resist her ample charms - not the long-legged caretaker with a pocketful of keys, whose obsession led to divorce, or the geography teacher, forced to resign when the headmaster caught him riding the fourteen year old like an ageing jockey. That last vigorous gallop lost him his job, pension and the chance of retaining his 'teacher of the year award'.

This final humiliation eventually confined him to a life of removing furniture, in contrast to Lorna, who soon had a white Mercedes and a villa in the South of France. Not bad for someone who left school with only two assets and a certificate for swimming a width.

Without opening my tired eyes, I could describe scenes in the billet as the usual panic began to set in. Stan struggling unsuccessfully to arrange his blankets into a liquorice allsorts effect, followed invariably by a spate of curses as they tilted to the side. Steve perfecting his locker layout, to ensure razor, shaving soap, toothpaste, toothbrush and face cloth were correctly aligned, against the distraction of Jock, parading naked whistling *Colonel Bogey*.

Only Leroy could enjoy the luxury of being ready and confident, allowing him to assist Timex, now finding it ever more difficult to cope with everyday pressures.

The early morning routine of curses and bodily noises meant you could almost put a name to a fart - not that I cared today as the pain and memory of the previous night overshadowed any concern for bullshit. Julie would probably never want to see me again, although I couldn't say the same about her father, who clearly enjoyed watching me make a complete idiot of myself.

Almost as an afterthought, my hand slid anxiously beneath the blankets. Apart from soreness and a tendency to wince with every breath, all appeared to be in working order, as could be seen from the height of the blankets. Lorna Brown still had a lot to answer for.

"You were late last night, Joe." Stan's voice lacked any real emotion as he fought a losing battle with his kit. "I suppose you were having it off with that tart from the pub."

"Oh, you mean the one who saved you from bleeding to death?"

I sat dejectedly on the bed, goose pimples like bee stings, painfully aware of the difficulty in trying to raise my legs. "For your information she's not a tart. Nymphomaniac? Yes."

Stan's curiosity overcame any desire to refold the blankets, or improve his appearance, thus putting him at risk of having a Lee Enfield rifle inserted up his arse. Having read about such women, even going to the trouble of researching the word in a public library, he still wasn't sure if you could actually recognise one in the street. "I don't know how you do it. First date and she turns out to be...." - he remembered the Oxford dictionary's definition - "a woman with excessive sexual desires."

Now it was my turn to be impressed. "You've obviously come across them before. Wish I'd known. You could've given me a bit of advice."

"Hardly the sort of thing you brag about."

"Well, at least it saves me boring you with all the gory details."

Stan nodded unconvincingly, not wanting to miss the opportunity of widening his limited knowledge of sexual abnormalities. "So, you managed it in the end?"

"Yes, several times - in fact I was relieved when she passed out."

"Bloody hell! This lot were asleep by ten."

"But not you?"

"No, I kept tossing and turning."

"Yes, Jock said he heard your bed springs going. Did you succeed in the end?"

Stan's normally ruddy complexion turned from a blush to a purple rage. "Why don't you mind your own fucking business?"

"What's the matter with him?" enquired the Scotsman, as Stan resumed his battle with the blankets.

"No idea, mate. All I did was ask about his sleep."

Jock sat beside me, carrying out the usual early morning inspection. "Do you think that vein's changing colour, Joe?"

I gave a cursory glance in the direction of his lap. "Looks perfectly normal to me."

He turned around hoping for a second opinion, until Steve put his mind at rest. "For God sake, there's nothing wrong with it. Why don't you put the bloody thing away?"

Jock wasn't entirely convinced but to everyone's relief he at least changed the subject. "So what happened between you and this barmaid?"

I bit down on my lower lip, trying to put last night's events into an acceptable sequence. "It began as an ordinary sort of night. Boy meets girl, girl meets boy."

"Boy shags girl." interrupted the blunt Scotsman, who had a way of simplifying even the most delicate of situations.

"We met in a pub if you must know, then we went for a walk. Afterwards she invited me back to meet her father - that was a shock."

"Why, did you know him?"

"No."

"Was he black?"

"How could he be black?"

"I bet there was something wrong with him."

"Why should there be anything wrong with him? If you must know he'd just completed twenty five years in the artillery."

"I asked if there was something wrong with him ... you said no."

There were times when Jock couldn't be ignored, and times when he could.

"Julie's old man knows all about Jenkins ... virtually admitted he had a hold over the CO. Apparently they went through the war together except the CO came out with all the glory, medals, citations, promotion. Jenkins came out with sweet FA other than a hold over the so-called war hero."

"No wonder he gets away with murder. So what can we do about it?" Steve's interest in planning the sergeant's downfall, failed to rub off on Jock.

"All we want to know is, did you give her a good seeing to, or what?"

At this point I had intended a blow by blow account of the beating, but it wouldn't exactly enhance my credibility. They were far more likely to be impressed by my successes with the opposite sex.

"That would be telling," I said. "All I can say is, she could scream for England."

"Didn't her old man say anything?" I'd forgotten his involvement. Steve obviously hadn't. "All that shouting and screaming?"

"Oh, he's ... deaf as a post. Listening to all those shells going off, I suppose."

Steve wasn't so easily brushed aside. "You did well to hold a conversation with him, then."

This was a difficult one to get out of - words wouldn't be sufficient, leaving no alternative but to distract their attention.

"Christ Almighty!" gasped Leroy, as my pyjama top came off.

"Fucking hell!" Stan began to have second thoughts about involving himself with a nymphomaniac. "Just look what she's done to him."

Within seconds, I was the main attraction, an exhibit to be gasped at and prodded as they inspected every bruise. Only Jock remained unimpressed.

"If the truth's known, he got drunk and fell down a flight of stairs."

"Are you sure her father didn't catch you?" Steve's poking extracted a loud wince.

"Pack it in. I'm sore enough without you lot making it worse."

"I hope it was worth it." Steve had the ability to put doubt in everyone's mind, except Stan's.

"You can't beat a bit of animal lust."

"Well, whatever turns you on." Steve no longer talked down to us, although he could still be cynically sarcastic. "Personally I'd sooner stick to women."

I moved away closely followed by the suspicious Scotsman. "No sign of any scratches or love bites."

"She is twenty not twelve."

"They look like punches to me. I bet you tried to rape her."

"Don't talk stupid, she's only half my size."

"In that case you should put her in the ring with Henry Cooper. She'd knock the shit out of him."

Timex watched and listened, irritation turning to anger and finally jealousy as he thought of Wendy. Not once had he considered another woman - even his fantasies concerned her, unlike every one else, lusting after anything remotely female.

Wendy had been the first to care, first to kiss him with any real passion, and first to see him naked as a man apart from a swimming baths attendant who came into the cubicle with sixpence in one hand and something frightening in the other. She was also the first to hold his quivering willy before guiding it lovingly into a place he was assured no one else had ever been.

Wendy always said he was beautiful but the mirror told a different story. Teeth reduced in number, which on occasions produced an embarrassing whistling sound, and a receding hairline, a legacy from his father who claimed it was a sign of virility. Even his body lacked symmetry. The stocky footballer's legs making his upper body appear somehow unconnected.

Perhaps she woke up one morning, suddenly aware of his faults. Perhaps she found someone without any.

The occasional pangs of doubt, usually placed there by one of us, never deterred him from extolling the virtues of fidelity. "I don't know how you can go with different women. You can't have much respect. I would never cheat on Wendy."

Although the comment referred to me, I had no intention of replying - unlike Jock. "I don't know why not, she's obviously cheating on you."

"I'd know if she was."

"Not from her, you wouldn't. She hasn't answered a bloody letter yet. Why don't you forget about her and enjoy yourself?"

"Like you, you mean?"

"At least I don't sit around moping, writing letters no bugger wants to read. You must be the most depressed and depressing sod the army has ever had the misfortune to recruit."

At this point in time the NAAFI appeared an attractive proposition compared to the alternatives - Jock reducing Timex to tears; cross-examination by Steve, or listening to Stan's epitaph for the recently deceased Clark Gable.

Visitors to the NAAFI were greeted by a life-size painting of a First World War officer waving a revolver as he ordered his troops out of the trenches and to their death. Underneath, the inscription, '*Over the top lads*'. To which had been added '*Goodbye, goodbye, I wish you all the last goodbye'*.

In an attempt to make us feel at home, the army had installed an American style jukebox containing the energetic works of Elvis Presley, Little Richard, Jerry Lee Lewis and Chuck Berry. Sadly, we were only allowed to feel at home between 6 and 8 p.m. on Fridays and Saturdays.

A small room opposite the gents contained a full-size snooker table, also with restricted time use and a ban on alcohol consumption.

Before I could move on, the lanky figure of Lance Bombardier Dodds came into view, carefully studying the position of the balls before bending over the table. His stance and cueing action suggested he spent a considerable amount of time in this room. Hard to believe that just a few hours earlier, this bastard had orchestrated a rather one-sided war.

I overcame the initial reaction to rush in and confront him, knowing my word against his wouldn't get me far. At school disputes were settled by fist fights, usually in the playground surrounded by over-enthusiastic classmates eager to congratulate whoever emerged victorious. The end came either with a bloody nose or intervention of a teacher, furious at being called out of a warm staff room.

Unfortunately this wasn't school and any thoughts of fair play ended there. But at least Dodds didn't have a monopoly on cunning, or the assistance of half-a-dozen regulars.

An adjoining storeroom contained everything for the cricketing enthusiast including a selection of bats made from the finest English willow. I chose one signed by Dennis Compton. Perhaps Lance Bombardier Dodds wouldn't feel so bad knowing he'd been hit by a top class bat.

His solo practice session continued, potting yellow, green and brown before snookering himself on the blue, at which point I crept through the half-open door, bringing the bat down heavily on the back of his unprotected head with enough force to have scored a six.

The NCO's face hit the green baize with a sickening thud; his right arm flopped sideways, knocking the black into a middle pocket. I did consider taking seven off his score but there wasn't time as I watched the cloth trying to absorb the growing circle of red. With a quick wipe of the handle, first lesson for any would-be assassin, I discarded the bat, hoping Compton wouldn't object to the imprint of his name on someone's head. Dodds clearly had a liking for tattoos, preferably ones of his own choosing in a place they could be seen without having to use two mirrors. Seconds later I joined a group of new recruits in the bar, laughing and joking as they bragged about their sexual conquests in an attempt to impress the middle-aged barmaid, smiling sweetly as she filled their glasses from the slop bucket. Not that it mattered, they probably couldn't tell beer from petrol unless someone lit a cigarette.

After ten minutes I assumed the lance bombardier had either breathed his last, in which case most of the snooker table would now be a grungy red, or he was on his feet, planning an ambush somewhere between the bar and gents. As a precaution I left by a rear entrance, rehearsing my alibi along the way. I could now officially claim to have beaten Lance Bombardier Dodds on the snooker table.

Thankfully the billet remained empty allowing more time to think of an acceptable explanation. In the meantime I could reflect on recent events - which may soon include ... murder. I certainly had no regrets, having always been a firm believer in an eye for an eye, the cane and capital punishment. The 'softly, softly' approach would never work in the current day's society.

Eventually thoughts of violence and revenge gave way to more tranquil ones, mainly concerning the fairer sex.

The army gave us paltry amounts of money, unpalatable food and a selection of clothes resurrected from the First World War - when all we really needed was women. So we dreamed about them. Timex thought about one woman, Stan worried about all women, while I fantasised with up to half-a-dozen. Some nights I had Marilyn Monroe, Rita Hayworth and Diana Dors. If I felt particularly energetic I would include Brigitte Bardot and Sophia Loren, to show I wasn't partisan.

With Lance Bombardier Dodds temporarily forgotten I thought about Clare, my first real love affair.

I was seventeen and gaunt looking, a taller version of Frank Sinatra whom she idolised and so I borrowed a grey Fedora hat worn at the same jaunty angle. She used to say without the bicycle clips and muffler there was a definite resemblance, inspiring me to practise singing, glass in one hand, cigarette in the other.

We met in the bleak lifeless period of winter, with everything under a blanket of snow. Long before white turned to green and the first daffodils opened their eyes I convinced myself she was the only girl for me.

Clare came from a wealthy background, never having to worry about money - whereas I learnt the value of it by never being allowed to have any. Her parents eagerly encouraged participation in everything from ballet to swimming, tennis to drama, all of them short-lived as her impulsive nature transferred to something new. Only later did it register when she replaced me with a painter and decorator who had his own van.

Never short on confidence, she had no hesitation in displaying her dancing skills or reciting Shakespeare. However, she derived her greatest satisfaction from riding horses, often panting faster than the horse when she returned from a ride.

Our long awaited bodily contact, following weeks of mounting frustration, occurred at a friend's eighteenth birthday party, when a national strike brought everything to a standstill, including the Dansette record player. Shirley Bassey's version of 'Kiss Me Honey Honey Kiss Me' slowed to a screeching halt. The unexpected darkness and shortage of chairs left Clare little option but to perch herself ladylike on my lap – quite disturbing for a young man with high levels of testosterone and flimsy underpants.

Two days later in the confines of her father's garden shed we consummated our relationship, amidst spades, forks, motor mowers and a large leather saddle which no doubt prompted her outburst - *ride me, ride me, you bastard, ride me.*

Our performance improved with practice, although I did draw the line when she asked me to wear the saddle.

In no time at all she wanted an engagement ring encrusted with diamonds - but I didn't have one on me at the time. I suggested a slightly longer courtship may be appropriate but she was impetuous and I was soon alone again.

Convinced she was calling my bluff, I played the rejected lover, hanging about in our familiar meeting places waiting for her to come looking. After six weeks of standing forlornly in shop doorways, collar turned up, hat pulled down, I caught pneumonia and the attention of a police officer who smiled sympathetically at my tale of unrequited love before charging me with loitering.

I wrote and told her I'd been arrested for robbing a wine store. She forwarded the name of her father's solicitor and a request for two dozen bottles of claret.

As a last resort I confronted the painter and decorator, only to discover he had a pregnant wife and violent temper. After I recovered, I began chasing his van on foot, shouting threats he couldn't hear from positions he couldn't see. During three weeks of running I wore out two pairs of pumps and shed a stone in weight, prompting my mother to inform the neighbours I was training for the marathon.

I gave up when I met Christine West, barmaid, flirt and would-be model. She spoke with a plum in her mouth and said 'sorry' every time I passed a comment. Eventually I developed a complex and stopped speaking to her. We survived in silence until Susannah came along, a plain-looking shop assistant with defective eyesight and a lisp. Her dowdy appearance and limited intellect not only improved my dented confidence, but also taught me relationships were not confined to sexual attraction.

Susannah's desire to remain undefiled was never really put to the test, particularly when she admitted a lack of interest in the male physique. Some while later she cleared off with her best friend, Jenny, setting up home together on the outskirts of Wolverhampton, selling dried flowers and herbs.

Judy had all the requisites to scale the social ladder - fashionable clothes, unending supply of hair lacquer, and the deportment of someone walking with a pencil clenched in the cheeks of their arse. To complete the picture she had a face bordering on beautiful, with eyes that challenged you to look away. Unfortunately, she came from Dudley, restricting her dreams of stardom to non-speaking roles.

Each of the girls had brought something a little different to our relationships, in addition to widening my knowledge of a female's hot spots, no-go areas and menstrual cycle. On the debit side they made hard work of my attempts to obtain a 40% pass mark in machine shop engineering.

My quiet period of reminiscing in the horizontal position, comforted by two pillows and a block of Cadbury's, ended abruptly with the return of Stan and Steve, anxious to update me on the latest incidents.

"Have you heard about Dodds?" Stan's animated expression confirmed it was bad news. "Some mad bugger's only half battered him to death." He sat beside me staring greedily at the chocolate. "When they led him out it reminded me of Marlon Brando in *On The Waterfront*. The one where he says, 'I could've been a contender, Charlie."

"Who's, Charlie?"

"His older brother."

"I didn't know Dodds had a brother."

Stan looked at the chocolate with longing, and me somewhere between disbelief and disgust. "I'm on about, Brando, not fucking Dodds. That scene where he gets beaten up and then has to walk up the gangway, eyes rolling, staggering all over the place. Well that's exactly how Lance Bombardier Dodds looked when they took him away. I've never seen so much blood."

"Does anyone know how it happened?"

Steve's intervention lacked Stan's enthusiasm. "It appears someone smashed his face in with a cricket bat. Now it's all out of shape."

"Surely that's not the only cricket bat?"

My sarcasm turned the Lancashire postman's forehead into a mass of wrinkles though they briefly disappeared when I offered him the last chocolate square. "Would you like a piece, mate?"

He couldn't have been more delighted had I offered him half share in a brothel. "Thanks, Joe." His outstretched hand remained empty as I popped the chocolate in my mouth.

"Ooooooops, sorry, mate."

"Bastard," he muttered, heading in the direction of his locker. "I have a box of ... Turkish delight, but you're not getting any."

"Now see what you've done." Steve's wry smile remained as he took Stan's place beside me. "Looks like pistols at dawn and no more film reviews. Now we shan't know who's shagging who."

I hadn't heard Steve use that word before, though I knew all about his interrogation methods.

"You didn't appear unduly surprised about Dodds, Joe?"

"I certainly won't be losing any sleep over him. Only a matter of time before someone had a swing at him."

"I think it was a little more than a swing, Joe. According to the medical orderly his face was a real mess..."

"No change there, then."

"... and will probably have to be rebuilt."

I felt no remorse, other than concern over the cricket bat and relief my fingerprints were no longer on it. "Well let's hope he doesn't kick the bucket."

"You didn't stay long in the NAAFI, Joe. Something crop up?"

"Yes, something cropped up. One of those rare opportunities you just have to take advantage of."

"And you managed to deal with it?"

"By all accounts, yes, mate."

"So long as it doesn't backfire."

"Why should it?"

"No reason so far as I'm concerned."

Having his thoughts confirmed put Steve's mind at rest and ended the interrogation. There would be no need to discuss the matter again.

Chapter 11

Sergeant Stockton moved his 25 stone bulk from behind a metal desk, the reinforced swivel chair creaked with relief as he transferred his weight to a large grey radiator. The worn carpet below indicated he spent most of his working day in that position.

Twice every year he proved his worth to the regiment by firstly anchoring the tug-of-war team to victory; simply leaning back on the rope and the by handing out presents to children dressed as a reluctant Father Christmas. The rest of the time he was an absolute liability, excused everything from parades to inspections, due to a shortage of uniforms for the fuller figure.

His current responsibilities were confined to administration - mainly dealing with complaints, filed under mislaid, and the management of married quarters, including the selection of suitable tenants, often more than willing to cross his palm with silver in order to improve their chances. Fortunately, he was a man of integrity who couldn't be swayed by money - although food hampers often did the trick.

'Fartarse' Stockton, earned his nickname in the mess where he regularly scoffed three helpings of everything on the menu - usually a sign to evacuate the building before he did the same with his bowels.

Before his fortieth birthday, the athletic looking sergeant excelled at football and rugby in addition to keeping his wife satisfied five times a week. Sadly, increasing body weight left him a spectator at all three.

"Right lads! I've got a little job for you." His piggy eyes, almost submerged by the surrounding fat flickered between the three of us.

"You're going to be working for Mrs Carter, the CO's wife."

Only Stan showed any real interest, no doubt due to the mention of someone female. "Doing what, Sarge?"

"No idea. She just asked for three strapping volunteers. Unfortunately, we couldn't find any, so you lot will have to do."

"I bet it's something highly confidential."

"A bit risky telling you then."

Sergeant Stockton glanced warningly towards the Scotsman. "Just remember who she is and treat her accordingly. Which means keeping your mouth shut and your eyes on the job."

"A bit of alright is she, Sarge?"

"She won't want anything to do with the likes of you."

The sergeant had mixed feelings regarding Mrs Carter, hating the way she viewed his obesity as though it were some form of disease. On more than one occasion he considered risking everything in order to wipe the contempt from her face as he showed the stuck-up bitch what a real man could do.

I sensed a little flattery might delay our departure. "Looks like you've got her weighed up, Sarge."

"When you've been around women as long as I have, lad, you get to read the signs."

Stan lifted his head in a hopeless gesture, almost thinking aloud. "Wish I could understand the buggers."

"Comes with experience, lad, comes with experience." He leaned briefly away from the radiator, a resounding boom releasing an obnoxious smell into the atmosphere. "I can tell you what they want, when they want it, and who they want it with."

"What about posh birds like Mrs Carter?"

Sergeant Stockton's face clouded over, chubby fingers tightening their grip on a silver-tipped biro. "They're usually the worst ... always on the lookout for a bit of rough ... someone who knows what it's all about. Not a half-baked pratt who doesn't know which end to piss from."

I decided his ego needed further massaging. Can't be easy trapped inside a body whose only function appears to be polluting the environment and frightening the children. "Come on, Sarge, tell us how you do it. What's the secret in pulling women?"

His gaze drifted towards the window as he began to relax. It wasn't often he had a captive audience. "I must admit I've had my share of women."

"But not recently," whispered Jock.

"Tall, short, fat, thin. Mothers, daughters..."

"Grandmothers?" Suggested Stan, but the sergeant wasn't listening. "Three in a bed, group sex. I even joined in with a couple of lesbians one time."

"Bloody hell!" exclaimed Stan, already reliving his favourite fantasy.

"I've always wondered what they got up to."

"Then there was Greta, a German Frau. Said I reminded her of Adolf."

"You look nothing like him. He was short and skinny with a moustache."

"Her husband."

Stan couldn't quite believe it. "You mean ... you were poking Hitler's wife?"

"For fuck's sake!" snarled the Scotsman. "Why don't you shut up and let him get on with it?"

The sergeant took a deep breath, unable to hide the smile as he continued his walk down memory lane. "French Mademoiselle's, Spanish Senorita's, and a feisty American dame who couldn't keep her hands off me." He left out the fact she was a law enforcement officer conducting a strip search following his arrest for suspected smuggling. "Oh, and black women, I'm quite partial to a bit of black every now and then." Clearly Sergeant Stockton didn't want to be accused of colour prejudice.

Stan raised a hand and I wondered what cosmopolitan flavour he could bring to the conversation. "Ever been to the Isle of Man, Sarge? We were there last year, absolutely full of crumpet. I remember this one tart from Liverpool, had tits like..."

"Gunner, I'm on about foreign places with beautiful women. Not a fucking day trip on the ferry with a scrubber from the corner shop." The sweat stains on Sergeant Stockton's faded khaki shirt began to enlarge along with his eyes, as memories of the past came flooding back.

"Then there was this Arab girl in Cairo ... said she'd never met anyone like me."

"We've said exactly the same, haven't we lads?" My interruption went unnoticed as the first hint of a leer crossed his face.

"She used to work as a dancer in one of those exotic clubs ... did a trick with a beer bottle. Now what was it called?"

"Watneys, Sarge?"

"The Pelican Club, that's it. First time I walked in our eyes met and you could almost feel the electricity between us."

Stan hung on every word. "Sounds like a scene from *Roman Holiday*, when Audrey Hepburn..."

"I stayed with her for three days and nights ... never slept a wink."

"Heavy snorer, was she, Sarge?"

The fat NCO sucked in his waist to 50 inches and then let it out to 60, accompanied by two shakes of the head and a loud sigh. "I'm on about sex, you arsehole … non-stop sex."

Jock's lips emitted a long, low whistle. "Christ! I bet that cost a fortune. They charge £5 an hour round our way."

Sergeant Stockton allowed himself a wry smile. "By the time I finish with them they're ready to pay me."

"I know what you mean, Sarge." Stan nodded sympathetically, recalling similar experiences. "It sometimes takes me ages."

"No, you fucking idiot! That's not what I meant."

"Sorry, Sarge. I just assumed …"

"Well you assumed fucking wrong." He eased his considerable bulk away from the hot radiator - further revelations would have to wait. "Now let's have you over to Mrs Carter's. And remember, it's yes, ma'am, no, ma'am. Show her the same respect as you would the CO."

"Do we salute her, Sarge?"

"Of course you don't fucking salute her! She's a civilian. What are you? Some sort of fucking imbecile?"

Getting annoyed came fourth behind smoking, sex and over-eating on the list of things he shouldn't do if he were to maintain his blood pressure somewhere between risky and mildly dangerous.

Sergeant Stockton silently considered the consequences and decided, having given up the first two, he could afford the luxury of indulging numbers three and four without fear of dropping dead. "Now get out of my sight and don't fucking come back."

Jock and I marched promptly from the office. Stan backed towards the door before producing a crisp salute.

The sergeant's reply came in the form of verbal abuse, closely followed by a heavy typewriter hurled with great force across the room, destroying the door and any chance he had of remaining calm.

"That salute was a good idea," mumbled the Scotsman as Stan caught us up. "Probably knocked five years off his life."

"Don't worry." My arm rested tentatively across the postman's shoulder, the way men do when they feel matey. "Ten minutes from now he'll be back in Cairo dreaming about dusky-skinned maidens and beer bottles."

The walk through married quarters reminded me of a run-down

council estate - badly in need of general improvements and the application of a fork and spade.

Cars in various stages of repair rested on bricks, bodies rusting, and interiors little more than a playroom for the kids. Wild eyed dogs, whose appearance gave no indication as to the breed of their parents, peered suspiciously through slatted gates, following our wearisome progress along a slight incline towards a dozen or so detached, executive-type houses, partly screened by a row of evergreens already shedding their cones.

Number one Maple Drive gave no outward information about the resident. In fact, the surrounding privet hedge, wildly overgrown, appeared to be the only sign of neglect in an otherwise immaculately-maintained cul-de-sac.

"I don't fancy cutting that with a pair of shears." Stan pushed open the garden gate, marching confidently along a crazy-paved path towards the CO's house. "I'd sooner clean that."

A black Daimler Conquest Century sat majestically in front of the garage, its appearance spoilt by the mud-splattered paintwork and dull chrome.

"I wonder if he wants a chauffeur?"

"Didn't know you could drive, mate."

Stan's look suggested it was a known fact. "I was brought up on the back of a tractor."

I joined him alongside the car, running my hand over the satin smooth metal. "Doesn't mean you can drive though, does it? I was brought up on a rocking-horse but I doubt I could ride a Grand National winner."

"Bollocks!" After flashing me a look of defiance he kicked the tyres, before heading towards the house, eyes staring straight ahead.

As we entered the open porch, he immediately began thumping the glass-panelled door with the flat of his fist. "There's no bugger in, we may as well piss off!"

"Give her a chance, mate. You know what women are when they're expecting someone important."

"Well she needn't bother on my account." He knocked once more, even trying the door handle before peering through the letterbox, emitting an appreciative whistle as he surveyed the interior. "There's a few quid's worth in here."

"Can I help you?"

Jock and I stood smartly to attention while Stan continued his appraisal of the contents.

"I wonder where they nicked that marble head of Nelson from?"

"It was a present from my husband, actually. Would you care to see the receipt?"

Stan turned crimson as he rushed to join us, struggling to come up with a plausible excuse. "I was just admiring your er.... bust." Only her eyebrows moved, the stony silence reduced Stan's ability to think and talk at the same time.

"When I said ... bust, I didn't mean your er ... things." Both hands cupped his chest in a desperate attempt to explain the comment. "I really meant, Nelson's. Not that there's anything wrong with yours." His voice faded as he considered the likely prospect of having to explain his remarks to her husband. "Er... sorry."

Mrs. Carter regularly suffered the inane babblings of young gunners without taking offence, except on one occasion when a young conscript with watery-blue eyes and a boil on his cheek thought he could get away with a playful pat on her much lusted after rear. Retribution came in the form of a stinging slap which burst the pus-filled swelling in a cascade of thick, yellowy green liquid, contaminating everyone within a three-yard radius. From that moment on randy young eyes never strayed below the level of her chin, even if the mind did.

"Well, are you going to say who you are? Or am I supposed to guess?"

"I'm Gunner Tramp, ma'am, and they're Gunners Clark and Strachan."

They came to attention one after the other but only Jock remembered Sergeant Stockton's words, nudging Stan sharply in the ribs.

"Put your arm down, you silly sod, you don't have to salute."

Mrs Carter's concern over protocol began to wane about the same time her husband suggested familiarising herself with chapter seven of the army manual - *Duties of an Officer's Wife*. "Well, shall we get on with it? Or are you just going to stand there?"

Lack of movement almost convinced her we were just going to stand there.

"Surely you've been informed of your duties?"

Three heads shook, increasing her irritation.

"I really haven't the time for this." She began to walk away, but paused after a few steps. "Well come along, I haven't got all day." Stan leapt into action, eager to make amends. Jock was in no way intimidated by her attitude.

"I thought she was talking to the fucking dog."

Three pairs of hungry eyes followed her shapely arse, hypnotized by the well-oiled movement as it bounced from side to side. If she realised the effect, it didn't show as she turned to face us.

"Could one of you cut that eyesore to a respectable level?" Long painted fingernails, refurbished every Tuesday morning at ten o'clock sharp by a mobile beautician with her own bike, pointed towards the overgrown privet hedge. "I could scream every time I look from the bedroom window."

"Your screaming days are over, ma'am. Gunner Clark will take care of that, he has very long arms."

"No I haven't."

"You will have by the time you finish."

Mrs Carter didn't care for my sense of humour, fixing me with the kind of stare that seemed to say 'keep this up and you'll be doing latrine duties for the next two weeks' but she continued, "And I want this Daimler cleaned inside and out. My husband will be using it for an official engagement tomorrow. The tools and gardening equipment are all in the garage."

She set off back to the house in that erect style, pushing strands of auburn hair away from her face as she beckoned me to follow. "This job is indoors."

I half-turned, but my knowing wink received the customary two finger salute from Stan, and Jock satisfied himself with a comment regarding my personal habits.

The house, like everything else in Marlene Carter's life, was merely a status symbol separating her from other wives who knew very little about her background. To them she remained a stuck-up cow, born into a privileged background. Even the Welsh accent had been all but eradicated, thanks to a speech therapist who not only left her sounding like the Queen, but also acting like one.

Young girls who grew up in the bleak, wind swept valleys of the Rhondda's during the post-war years were expected to marry miners, produce half-a-dozen kids, and settle in a two up, two down terrace, with a communal toilet twenty yards away. Marlene Jones had no intention of becoming another victim so she moved to London where her newly acquired accent and undoubted beauty soon began to turn heads - none quicker than that of Colonel Carter who wooed her with tales of bravery, family connections, and the promise of financial security. Love never came into it - lust occasionally did but only until his heavy drinking reduced that to a failed attempt every few months, which no doubt accounted for her obvious frustration.

"When you've finished stock taking perhaps we can get on."

"Sorry, I was just admiring the oak-cased grandfather clock. I bet you're really proud of that."

"It's only a clock." She remained unimpressed with my comments. "It doesn't even keep good time."

She led me from the hall to a twelve-foot square side room, empty apart from a roll of carpet held together by sticky, black tape. "Can you fit this - it's been laying there for nearly a month."

I wanted to remind her carpet should always be unfolded but I knew she wouldn't be interested. "I'm not exactly a carpet fitter."

Mrs. Carter didn't want a discussion, emphasising the point with a deep sigh. "Can you do it, or not?"

My lack of confidence in fitting anything that didn't rely on micrometers, and my delay in answering, used up what little patience she had.

"Oh, I can't stand here all day." Her sudden departure left the decision to me, so I decided to 'Have A Go' as Wilfred Pickles would say. She obviously wasn't concerned - why should I worry about it?

Armed with a knife, scissors and a cloth measuring tape missing the first three inches, I pulled and kicked the brown Axminster into position before trimming off the edges which went into an old cardboard box advertising the name of the CO's favourite whisky. The whole thing took well over an hour and the experience ruled out any future career ambitions in that direction.

After straightening my aching back with enough facial distortions to have secured first place at a Butlin's gurning competition, I crossed to the bay window anxious to see how the others were progressing.

Stan, already halfway along the hedge, stood precariously on a ladder clipping furiously with a pair of squeaking garden shears. Unfortunately, his perception of horizontal didn't quite match his enthusiasm. Reducing the privet hedge from a starting height of eight foot to less than six, I estimated, at this rate of descent, he would finish the job on his knees.

Jock was equally industrious, using a green-coloured hosepipe to wash the car. Personally I thought it would be better with the windows closed but we all have our own way of doing things and the Scotsman wasn't known for accepting advice.

"Oh! I see you've done it." I could smell the drink even before I turned, and was aware the hostility had left her voice. Even the clothes were different: the tailored suit of earlier now replaced by a loose-fitting, lilac coloured housecoat, the bottom three buttons undone to reveal a large expanse of thigh.

"You've done an excellent job. I shall have to hire you again." The comment didn't require an answer so I didn't offer one, conscious she was probably naked beneath the fleecy garment. If further proof were needed a pair of pointed nipples came into prominence, either caused by the cold.... or something else.

Mrs Carter stood in the doorway, adopting a pose Stan would instantly compare to Dorothy Lamour or Betty Grable - except they didn't have the remnants of a Welsh accent, which always surfaced after three or four drinks. "I wonder how the others are getting on?"

"Well, the hedge is just about finished and the car should be dry in about half-an-hour, although inside may take a little longer."

She wasn't listening, just using the wall for support while she considered the next topic of conversation. "Awful thing about Lance Bombardier Dodds. Only playing snooker, I believe."

"I know, there are some terrible losers about."

"My husband thinks it was someone with a grudge ... probably a young soldier who doesn't like being ... er..."

"Bullied." I reminded her, trying to keep my eyes focussed above the neck, still unsure of her motives.

"He's a single man, I believe?"

"Yes, that's right. No family, no friends," - I paused to emphasise the punch line - "and definitely no parents."

Marlene Carter's concern over the unfortunate lance-bombardier quickly evaporated as she moved her weight from one foot to the other, making no attempt to cover her thigh. "Where are you from, gunner?"

"Wolverhampton."

She screwed her nose up and then hiccupped. "Sorry."

I wasn't quite sure which she was apologising for so I wisely let it pass. "I suppose you have a lot to do being the CO's wife?"

"Oh, yes, there's never a dull moment." The sarcasm returned accompanied by a look of resignation as she considered her situation. "The other wives avoid me like the plague, while their husbands are equally suspicious, frightened to look, never mind speak. She moved slowly forward, bare feet leaving clear indentations on the newly laid Axminster. "It's like living in a goldfish bowl. Plenty of time, but nothing to do."

I couldn't quite see the connection as she closed the distance between us, reducing my confidence with every step. It's one thing fantasising over the CO's lady in the darkest part of your mind - quite another when she's standing before you, warm and inviting, about to say something that could have a profound affect on your life.

"I'd find a job, except there's not much call for a full-time flower arranger."

The remark halted any temptation to take her in my arms and fondle those erect nipples - as did the follow up.

"No one realises the difficulties in being married to a CO. Everyone thinks it's a bed of roses."

Comparing her life with Ma's ruled out any show of sympathy. "I'm sure you have lots of other talents."

For some reason she took my comment as a compliment, allowing herself a wistful look as she tried to remember what they were. "Did have, you mean. Now they're all gone. I'm never invited out, except to boring regimental engagements, where I have to sit and smile while my husband makes the same speeches and cracks the same jokes that weren't even funny the first time. Of course everyone laughs because he's the commanding officer. Some days I could scream, I really could."

Clearly screaming was her way of letting off steam - something she did with increasing regularity and volume, much to the disgust of a husband, whose upbringing allowed him to control such emotional outbursts.

"Maybe you need to let your hair down once in a while."

My suggestion did nothing to improve her mood or expression. "Not much chance of that. I'm the CO's wife, remember. One foot out of place, I'd be confined to quarters for six months." She half-covered another burp. "I really shouldn't drink so much."

"Then why do you?"

"Dulls my senses, I suppose. Stops me thinking too much. Anyway

I shouldn't be talking to you like this." She moved towards the door, pausing for what could be a warning about over-familiarity. "Can I call you back ... say sometime next week?"

Her stance emphasised the fullness of her breasts, one milky-white thigh still on display. "I need the spare room carpeted by Friday."

"I'm at your service, ma'am. Ready, willing and able."

Her response didn't exactly curl my toes, in fact the raised eyebrows warned against further frivolous remarks.

"It's just to fit a bedroom carpet, nothing to get excited about. Now, if you don't mind, I have things to do ... perhaps you can let yourself out."

I suspected another drink was on her agenda, probably the only way she could get through each day - leaving me to contemplate what might have been.

Mrs Carter disappeared upstairs just minutes before Stan and Jock came banging on the front door.

"I've done the hedge, Joe."

"Yes, I've noticed. Never mind it'll soon grow again."

"Is there anything else to do?"

Jock gave him a push. "What are you asking him for? He's only the same as us."

"He knows I've got influence, mate."

"You've probably sat on your arse while we've been working."

He adjusted the position of his testicles with a grimace we all knew well. "I bet you didn't get anywhere with this one."

I waited until his hands reappeared, knowing it was simply a matter of time before they found another part of his anatomy to interfere with. "We got on like a house on fire. Believe it or not we have a lot in common."

"Alright, name something."

There were times when I admired the Scotsman's straight talking and persistency - unfortunately, this wasn't one of them. "We have the same star sign and we both enjoy classical music. In fact she's invited me back."

"Fuck off! She wouldn't look at you in a month of Sundays."

"Why not?"

He thought long and hard, hands returning to his testicles for inspiration. "Because she wouldn't, that's why."

Stan lost interest in the grandfather clock, preferring to give us the benefit of his experience. "Older women like Mrs Carter are always on the lookout for a young stud ... someone who can make them laugh."

"You mean like you?"

"Well, I do make women laugh."

"Yes, but you have to strip off to do it."

"Don't get on to me because you've ruined the CO's car."

"What about you with that hedge? It's like a bloody big dipper."

I pushed them apart, aware we were still in the hall surrounded by expensive fittings. "Why do you think she wanted me in the house?"

The Scotsman tried to include logic in his reasoning. "Because you were the only bugger left."

"No, because there was this chemistry between us, I felt it straight away. The moment our eyes met, we both knew."

"Knew what?"

"Something would happen."

Jock's cross-examination stuttered to a halt with Stan's timely intervention. "It's like a scene from *Brief Encounter*, with Trevor Howard and Celia Johnson. That began the same way."

"Don't start that film shit again. He'll be telling us next they're getting married."

"It's a bit premature to be thinking about marriage, mate." My voice dropped to little more than a whisper, encouraging them both to lean closer. "The problem is, she wants to see more of me -when the CO's out of course. Wouldn't like him to know what's going on ... that would make promotion difficult."

"Bloody hell!" Stan's look of surprise quickly turned to envy as he considered the possibility. "He must be giving her one."

"He's pulling your plonker. She's probably been out all the time."

"Well I didn't see her leave." Stan confirmed his evidence with the gravity of Sherlock Holmes solving another murder. "And the cars still on the drive. Mind you she'd need a wet suit to drive that bloody thing."

"At least it'll be dry by tomorrow but that fucking hedge will never be the same again."

"Whatever's going on down there?"

Mrs Carter stepped unsteadily on to the landing, unbuttoned housecoat revealing most of her legs and everybody's immediate attention.

"Fucking hell!" mumbled the Scotsman, right hand dropping instinctively towards the groin area.

"Christ Almighty!" Stan leant slightly forward, neck bulging red as it strained upwards. "It reminds me of the way Marilyn Monroe stood over that grating in *The Seven Year Itch*. You could see right up her..."

I shoved him aside. "Sorry, Mrs Carter ... we were just leaving."

"I bet that's buggered your wedding plans." Jock found the whole thing amusing but Stan was unable to tear his eyes away.

"I don't think she's wearing any..."

My hand clamped over his mouth, forcing the lips inwards in an attempt to stifle further excitement. "Right then, we'll be off. Don't forget to let me know when you want me to ... come again."

Mrs Carter tried to make sense of it all, staring down with the expression of someone not quite sure what was going on, her auburn hair almost covering her face. A long pause eventually refreshed her memory, indicated by a slight nod as she got us in focus. "Oh, yes. The sooner the better, you know how desperate I am."

I winked at them both before marching out, knowing they would immediately follow.

"I don't know how you do it." Stan drew level, unable to keep the admiration out of his voice as he considered his spartan sex life. "We can't get a bloody look in ... you've already had the local barmaid and now the CO's wife. At this rate you'll get through every female in Gravesend and quite a few in the rest of the country."

Jock brought up the rear, kicking out at anything not cemented in. "He'll be fucking the Queen next."

This latest experience elevated my position, at least in Stan's eyes as he tried to widen his knowledge of the opposite sex. "Is she any different from ordinary women?"

"Yes, you have to do everything by numbers, in two three, out two three, fire two three and then light a cigarette."

"But you don't smoke, Joe."

My arm settled affectionately around the postman's shoulders as I realised how naive he really was. "Sometimes we have to do things we may not always agree with ... but if it makes other people happy."

Jock couldn't contain himself any longer, fuming at the way my luck appeared to be progressing compared to his. "Ain't it fucking marvellous? We do all the work while he's in there giving her one. Jammy bastard! I bet you never gave us a fucking thought."

"Yes, I did, but then I thought, this is no time to start laughing."

"Come on, Joe." urged Stan, anxious to hold my attention. "Tell us what it was like. Did she scream and shout?"

"Only when she looked through the window and saw that fucking hedge. Fortunately, I was able to distract her. The things I do to save a mate."

"Thanks, Joe."

"What are you thanking him for, you silly sod? We've done all the fucking work while he's sat on his arse."

Jock had all the skills of a regular soldier. He could fart at the most inappropriate time, belch before or after meals, spit great distances and curse with enough feeling to impress a Shakespearean teacher. He could also crack his knuckles to the tune of Colonel Bogey - something he decided to do as he stood defiantly before me.

"I suppose you were doing me a good turn as well?"

"No, I was doing her a good turn and you a favour."

"Bollocks!"

Chapter 12

"Hands off your cocks and onto your socks."

The voice of Bombardier Hawkins received a response other NCOs could only dream about. The words were a little predictable but they had the desired effect, catapulting pyjama-clad bodies from beneath warm, comforting blankets, showing all the signs of a frustrated nights sleep. Even Jock dispensed with the usual lewd display, not wishing to incur the Bombardier's wrath at 5:15 on a cold November morning as he reluctantly joined five other sex-starved young gunners, most having spent yet another night either reliving childhood crushes or inventing ones.

I would have been about nine or ten when Miss Talbot came into our lives, employed by the local junior school to assist anyone with learning difficulties. Within two days every lad in the class confessed to having this problem with quite a few asking for extra tuition. She also had a smile that could turn legs to jelly and a way of capturing attention that was never taught at Teachers' Training College.

During lessons she would walk around the classroom humming the hit of the year - *I'd Like to Get You on a Slow Boat to China* prompting one ten year old to substitute the word 'Get' for one the older boys were beginning to use in every sentence. It didn't rhythm, but at least it was more in line with our feelings.

Miss Talbot invariably wore high heel shoes, one strap over the front, stockings, suspenders and skirts that would ride up over her knees. We used to fight for the front row seats just feet away from her elevated desk, allowing us the opportunity to further our education, but not in the academic sense.

The view between her legs proved far more informative than any English lesson. Soft pink flesh peeping above nylon-clad thighs, leading to tufts of black crinkly hair sprouting from each side of flimsy knickers that were changed every single day. Those on the front row would sit through an entire lesson with only one hand visible as they fantasised over thoughts of what existed at the top of Miss Talbot's legs. She was the reason most of us failed our eleven plus and became ambidextrous.

The sudden arrival of Bombardier Hawkins interrupted our daydreams as we tried to figure out the reason for this early start. War could be ruled out. No-one with any sense would start at this unearthly hour. No, it had to be something far more serious - perhaps the milkman had overslept or the cook had mislaid the tin opener.

Hawkins strode purposefully between unmade beds, his razor sharp creases and highly polished boots contrasting sharply with our crumpled pyjamas as we stood to attention. Three degrees of frost reminded us of the need to keep our blood circulating.

"Stand fucking still! You're like a troop of performing seals. The next one to shiver will be parading outside."

I wondered if goose pimples were against army regulations because we were all afflicted by them.

"Just look at yourselves." Only Stan took up the invitation, staring down at the bristling state of his skin with a look of revulsion. "Bloody hell! I must be allergic to something."

"Well it can't be work, boy, you never fucking do any. Now stop moving about and keep your eyes to the front." His head shot back as if preparing himself for the arrival of Winston Churchill. "Now listen to me - this is important."

So it was the tin opener!

"I'm after the bastard who did for Lance Bombardier Dodds...and when I find him..."

His unfinished threat left us in no doubt the consequences would be extremely painful, if not illegal.

"You lot were the only ones on a free period at that time, which makes you the chief suspects."

The news failed to extract a confession - just a brief explanation of the law according to Gunner Clifford. "Excuse me, Bombardier! But the fact that one or all of us visited the scene of the crime hardly constitutes an admission of guilt."

Five heads nodded in agreement. Unfortunately, Bombardier Hawkins wasn't one of them.

"This isn't a fucking court of law and you're not the judge and jury. I am. So I will decide who's fucking guilty - got it?"

We all accepted his definition of justice, none more so than Timex, whose over-enthusiastic nodding caused his pyjama trousers to slide downwards, covering his feet and ankles but very little else.

"Leave them!" screamed the Bombardier as the blushing Welshman began to bend. "This isn't a fucking fashion show."

Five steps, each one increasing the sardonic sneer, brought him within touching distance of the embarrassed gunner. "What about you, Thomas ... you got the balls to do it?"

His lack in providing an urgent answer gave Bombardier Hawkins the opportunity to find out for himself, using a clammy right hand. "You'd better answer, boy, or I'll twist the buggers off."

The brief army career of Gerry Dylan Thomas, named after the poet whom he had absolutely nothing in common with, continued to be a humiliating experience. "No, Bombardier."

"Are you sure, boy?"

The tightening grip produced beads of perspiration on the Welshman's wrinkled forehead as he resisted the urge to cringe. "Definitely, Bombardier."

A final squeeze widened the sneer, before Hawkins moved sideways to confront another anxious looking gunner. "Mr fucking Lawman, maybe you know who did it? Don't worry, they'll get a fair trial ... I'll see to that."

"Sorry, Bombardier. I've no idea."

"But you would say if you knew?"

Steve's capacity for lying, that essential ingredient for any prospective lawyer, had improved dramatically over the past few weeks. "Yes, Bombardier."

"You're a fucking liar, boy! What are you?"

Steve weighed up the consequences of remaining silent, including the possibility of having his private parts mangled.. No one had ever touched him down there, although a priest had come pretty close after he confessed to feelings of guilt each time he masturbated. 'Perhaps you're not doing it right,' replied the flushed priest, reaching out a sweaty palm. 'Let me show you how I do it!'

"I'm a fucking liar, Bombardier."

Having achieved another humiliating victory, the sadistic NCO came face to face with suspect number three. "What about you, Clark? Think you could beat someone's brains in?"

Stan gave the question serious consideration, knowing a 'yes' would leave him open to further questioning, which may have painful repercussions. On the other hand, 'no' could dent his recently acquired reputation as someone you don't mess around with. "I don't really know, Bombardier."

"I don't really know, Bombardier," mimicked the smirking NCO. "What sort of a fucking reply is that?"

The Lancashire postman always managed to appear guilty, a failing that dogged him through school, leading to numerous encounters with the headmaster's cane. "I er ... don't think I could do it." Stan held his breath. Having risked his reputation in order to satisfy the Bombardier's, he now resorted to praying - but the appeal fell on deaf ears when long thin fingers wrapped themselves firmly around his cold nose.

"You're a fucking nancy boy, Clark. What are you?"

He tried desperately to co-operate but the fingers tightened their grip, stifling any hope of a response as they pressed bleeding gums against teeth already crooked, thanks to his slow reactions while keeping wicket for the post office cricket team.

"Are you fucking deaf, boy?"

Stan shook his head as the pain made him squirm, bending at the knees in an attempt to escape. But the fingers wouldn't let go and the Bombardier's contorted face moved closer. "Answer me, boy, or I'll twist it off."

Gunner Clark obliged, not too clearly but enough to satisfy his assailant who promptly let go with a final yank. Stan fell clumsily to the floor in a tangle of arms and legs - blood continuing to dribble from the corners of his mouth on to pyjamas used to different kinds of stains.

Jock tried to convince himself he wouldn't stand for that kind of treatment having faced far meaner bastards than Hawkins - except they never had two stripes for protection.

"What about you, Strachan? That's your sort of style ... attacking an unarmed man, isn't it?"

Young men brought up in the rough parts of Glasgow never really developed a sense of fair play, so the insult went unheeded. "Don't know anything about it, Bombardier."

"I don't like you, Strachen. You're a fucking wanker."

Jock resisted the urge to pass any comment that would aggravate the situation, having been called far worse during his stint at Macgregor's nightclub. "Not many people do," he agreed.

Bombardier Hawkins had a lot in common with the Scotsman. Not many people liked him either. But there was easier prey. He confronted Leroy, unable to hide his dislike for anyone with a dark skin. "You were in the NAAFI about the time this happened, Farley."

His first real piece of evidence failed to alter Leroy's rather subdued expression. "I did visit the NAAFI, yes."

"And you were seen leaving in a hurry."

"I had something to do."

"By all accounts you did it ... battering the lance Bombardier with a fucking cricket bat."

"No, Bombardier."

"You've complained on previous occasions, haven't you, Farley?"

Leroy chose to remain silent, an unwise decision given the close proximity of Hawkins' stick.

"Answer the question, you black bastard!"

The years of racial taunts taught Leroy the folly of showing any reaction, even when the stick cracked ominously against his head.

"I'll beat a fucking answer out of you if I have to."

A trickle of blood ran down his cheek, but I could see the lad wasn't about to break his silence, even if I was.

"We've all complained at one time or another."

His startled expression gave me the opportunity to continue. "I was also in the NAAFI when the incident happened, so were a dozen others."

Hawkins' stick reached me before he did, jolting my head back with a series of vicious prods. "I'm getting sick of you, boy. Always shoving your fucking nose in. What's the matter? One beating not enough?"

Only two of us in the room knew of my scuffle with Dodds and his henchmen, not that I did much scuffling. "I was simply trying to point out - he's not the only suspect. The Lance Bombardier must have more enemies than Adolf Hitler."

"Including you, Tramp."

The end of his stick fitted snugly into my left nostril preventing any kind of head movement without risk of permanent damage. "I must admit he's not my favourite person."

Hawkins felt the advantage slipping away as my unwavering gaze convinced him a change of tactics may produce better results. "Stand at ease!"

We all relaxed except Gunner Thomas who wasted no time in returning his pyjama trousers to their original position. This change of heart, including the benefit of a half smile, gave no indication of the Bombardier's hastily assembled plan of retribution.

"Let's hope one of you sees sense in the next few days and owns up because, it not, I'll make your fucking lives a misery."

We waited for news of our uncertain future, no longer relaxed as he glowered at each of us in turn.

"In order to complete basic training and pass out, you have to run five miles in under an hour. Normally it doesn't matter - but in this instance you will not do either until you succeed. Which means you could be here for months. In fact we can arrange that your two years lasts forever."

Both hands disappeared behind his back, returning after a few seconds as he conjured up even more problems. "Oh, by the way … you'll be doing it with full pack, rifles, tin hats, the lot. It just needs one of you to fail and you'll all have to do it again the next day, and the day after that. In fact every fucking day until somebody confesses."

"You can't do that - it isn't fair." Steve's comment simply widened the Bombardier's grin.

"Sergeant Jenkins can. He runs this fucking camp, or hadn't you noticed?" The grin vanished in an instant. "Any objections, take them up with him."

"I can't run five miles, Bombardier," admitted Timex. "I never could at school."

"Oh, dear! What a shame. You're not going to be very popular then, are you, Thomas?"

The smug expression remained as he headed for the door, pausing, one foot in mid-air, as I called his name. "Bombardier Hawkins! It was me, I battered Dodds. Not that he didn't deserve it - the man's a bloody psychopath."

Hawkins silently congratulated himself before turning with a movement lacking the usual noise and precision. "I knew it was one of you bastards. Just a matter of time. Better start packing boy … you won't be coming back here again. You're bloody lucky it didn't end up a murder charge - still might if the poor sod dies."

"Do you want me to pack, Bombardier?" Leroy waited till the NCO transferred his gaze.

"This isn't kindergarten, Farley. You can't go with him. The man's a fucking criminal ... he's just admitted it."

"That was to save me. Joe didn't beat up Dodds, I did."

Bombardier Hawkins glanced from one to the other as the first sign of doubt increased his frown. "Don't piss me about! Which one of you did it?"

Jock beat everyone to it, arm shooting aloft in a pose reminiscent of Hitler acknowledging his troops. "Neither of them, bombardier - they haven't got the guts. It was me."

Just seconds ago that third stripe had looked a foregone conclusion. Now the bastards were playing him for a fool, even putting the hard-earned second stripe at risk. "Anyone else want to risk a fucking prison sentence? Or is it just the three stooges?"

He looked around for the faintest hint of a smirk, but everyone remained grim-faced, having learnt the errors of displaying any kind of pleasure. "You bastards want to stick together ... you'll fucking suffer together"

Six pyjama-clad bodies, hands and feet devoid of feeling maintained their eyes at regulation height, awaiting the outcome of Bombardier Hawkins threat.... "Parades and inspections on the hour every hour, around the clock." The realisation he too would suffer prompted a few hurried amendments .... "starting at six, finishing at ten o'clock. And don't forget those five-mile runs. You could be the longest serving national servicemen in fucking history."

The expected protests never materialised so he made a tactical withdrawal.

Silence and concern followed his departure, both of them broken by Stan's confusion. "What does he mean, longest serving national servicemen?"

"He's already explained." Steve's reluctance to elaborate fell on deaf ears.

"So, what does he mean?"

"I assume he'll keep us on some trumped-up charge until the matter's resolved ... none of which will reduce our two years."

Stan remained unsure, turning towards the Scotsman. "What does he mean?"

"Oh, for Christ's sake! It means none of this time will count."

His pyjama trousers hit the floor. "If the shitbag keeps us here for an extra month, we'll have to do two years and a month. One or two thicko's, have been known to serve nearly three years."

Jock bent forward, the first sign of concern entering his voice as he assessed the effects of the cold. "Bloody hell! It's shrunk." The worrying discovery wrinkled his brow. "What do you think, Steve?"

The would-be-lawyer never felt inferior to Jock except on these occasions. "I wish you'd put the sodding thing away. We're all sick of looking at it."

We dressed in silence, each with our own thoughts: mine focussing entirely on the predicament they were all under because of me. Expecting everyone to suffer for my actions left me no choice but to confess. "Look lads, there's something you should know. I really did batter Dodds."

The shocked reaction failed to materialise, obviously they were going to take a little more convincing. "Did you hear what I said?"

"Yeah, yeah, yeah," replied Jock, having transferred his interest to a blackhead, which he ejected with thumb and forefinger. "Now tell us something we didn't know."

"He's right, Joe." Steve's explanations were never simple and straightforward, one of the qualities required to enter chambers. "Having considered the evidence, we came to that conclusion by a process of elimination. But don't worry, you have our full support, doesn't he lads?"

A chorus of agreement failed to convince me this was right. "I appreciate what you're doing - but there's no need for everyone to suffer."

Stan pulled on the last sock, head remaining in the down position. "Joe's got a point."

"Shut up and get dressed," snapped Leroy. "We're all in this together so you may as well get used to it. Anyway, what's a five mile run amongst friends?"

"It's a bloody long way," I reminded everyone. "Especially carrying all that junk. Be hard enough in shorts and pumps."

"Save your breath, Joe. There's nothing you can do about it."

"Sooner or later I'll have to confess … may as well do it sooner rather then later."

The Welshman sensed a way out, hoping Stan at least would support him. "Joe's talking a lot of sense." The hostile reaction hardly encouraged him to pursue the suggestion, changing his outlook from positive to negative. "You would all succeed without me."

No-one contradicted Gunner Thomas, who couldn't run or jump unless an officer appeared - and then he could do both better than anyone else. "But what can I do?"

"Fucking desert!" Jock's hand disappeared once more and I wondered what the problem could be. "That would solve everything."

"As a matter of interest," - Steve's voice always had serious undertones - "if someone in the billet commits suicide, the others are automatically discharged." Turning to Timex. "Not that I'm suggesting it as a solution."

"Why not?" Enquired Stan, already planning an early return to the Post Office. "Get Joe out of a hole."

"Do you still get discharged if you murder someone?"

Steve considered the Welshman's question with all the gravity of a judge about to pass a life sentence. "Yes, I believe so ... but you don't get the pension."

"This suicide business," enquired Stan, still seeking a way out. "Does it apply to anyone?"

Timex didn't wait for the question to be clarified, directing his anger at the sea of hopeful faces. "You needn't look at me - I'm not committing suicide."

"Why not?" asked Jock, "How many times have you said you don't want to live without Wendy? Now here's your chance. No point carrying on now she's pissed off with somebody else."

"Forget it."

"Only takes a few seconds and you won't feel a thing ... right lads?"

"We can almost guarantee it," agreed Stan optimistically. "One minute you'd be here, the next...you wouldn't."

"The answer's no, how many more bloody times?"

"You probably need more time to think about it ... after all it is a big decision." Jock remembered the time old Mrs Butler ran screaming from the flat next door, having found her husband hanging from the roof by his braces. He was still going up and down when the ambulance men arrived, shaking their heads as they lowered his body onto a stretcher. Memory of this put a little more compassion into his voice.

"What if we made it worth your while? You know ... all chipped in a few quid. You could die a rich man."

"And we'd take care of all the arrangements," assured Stan. "You wouldn't have to do a thing."

"That's the least we can do for a mate," added the Scotsman solemnly.

"Do you honestly believe I would commit suicide just to get you lot out of the army?"

"Well if you're going to die anyway, what does it matter? At least you'd be dying for a reason." Stan pondered his statement. "You'd be remembered as a martyr, like Joan of Arc or James Dean."

"They didn't commit suicide. She burnt at the stake, he died in a fucking car crash."

Timex continued shaking his head. "I can't believe I'm hearing this. At first I thought you were joking - but you're actually serious."

The Scotsman's expression wavered between hurt and surprise. "Death's no joking matter, especially when it's a…friend."

"Friend? Fucking friend? You must be sick … both of you."

He slammed shut the locker door and I could feel the tension as my right arm settled on his shoulder. "Just calm down, mate. You don't have to do anything… not if you don't want to."

"Of course I don't bloody want to." He knocked my arm away, no longer prepared to discuss the suggestion rationally. "I'm off for breakfast - fuck the lot of you."

"What an ungrateful bastard." Stan's disappointment showed itself in the hastily folded envelope of blankets. "You try to help somebody and what do you get?"

"Fucking insults - nothing but fucking insults."

I waited until the two instigators recovered from the shock of rejection. "Well, you certainly made him feel wanted."

Jock's grin confirmed it was all a game - but not to the ruddy-faced former postman. "Now what have we done?"

"Don't you think he's got enough problems without you two making them worse? He's already struggling to cope, worried sick about Wendy, and then you come along talking about suicide. Why don't you join him for breakfast? Try and cheer the poor sod up. Tell him it was all a wind-up."

"But it wasn't." Stan's defiance began to crumble. "Anyway why should we have to do it?"

"Because you're the buggers who depressed him in the first place." Steve, as always the peacemaker, placed his beret at a jaunty angle, pushing the remains of his hair under with one finger. "Come on, let's go and see what we can do."

Leroy and I remained behind, our day on the rota to buff the floor and do all the other things apron-clad females do so proficiently.

"I don't know what Ma would say if she could see me now. I bet your mother wouldn't be too impressed."

"No idea." The half-hearted shrug suggested he didn't really care. "Haven't seen her for years."

"You must've left home early."

"Not early enough." A long pause stretched out an explanation "I could never understand why other parents wouldn't let their kids have anything to do with me. She said it was because of my colour ... was it buggery!"

I remained silent, not wishing to interrupt his flow.

"She used to bring a different bloke back every night. I had more uncles than the rest of the kids put together. They used to paint 'Scrubber' and 'Slag' on the front door. The first time I caught her at it I was physically sick - can you believe that?"

My expression remained sympathetic, trying to come up with something that would make him feel better. "I felt pretty much the same after creeping in to my parents bedroom late one Christmas eve to see if Santa Claus was coming. He wasn't, but my mother certainly was. I couldn't face her for months ... it must've been a hundred times worse for you."

I tried to keep the conversation going without sounding too nosey. "How long did this go on for?"

"Until the council took me away. Said I needed proper care so they shoved me into a home where the bastard in charge was a known child-abuser. Can you believe that? I've seen kids of ten and eleven trying to commit suicide." He anticipated my next question, pausing only long enough to satisfy himself the room was empty. "If you managed to run away the police would bring you back to another beating and no food for a week."

His story reminded me of the street urchin in Oliver Twist. I was about twelve when I became familiar with the antics of Bill Sykes, Fagin and the Artful Dodger. But that was in Victorian times - not the 1950's. "Surely there was someone you could turn to ... friends, relatives?"

Leroy's expression told me things weren't quite so simple. "What friends and relatives? Nobody wanted to know ... still don't. Anyway who's going to take notice of a young black kid with a chip on his shoulder?" He no longer tried to disguise the bitterness in his voice. "You can't explain to anyone unless they've suffered a similar experience. The loneliness, fear and despair, knowing not one person in the whole fucking world gives a toss what happens to you."

I waited for him to calm down a little, knowing another word out of place could jeopardise further revelations, but eventually impatience forced me to give him a gentle reminder. "What happened next, mate? I mean, how did you get away?"

His delay in responding suggested the confession may either be about to end or serialised on a daily basis, in direct competition with Dick Barton, Special Agent.

"I've never spoken of this to anyone, Joe."

"Sometimes it's better to get things off your chest, mate."

"Why? It's taken me years to get over it. What's the point in bringing it all up again?"

I couldn't quite think of one and I realised the others would be back soon. "Well, you've told me half the story, may as well finish it off ... unless you've shut the rest out of your mind."

His eyes temporarily closed, as if the memories were too painful. "I wish it were that easy. Occasionally I can shut it out until something or somebody triggers it off."

"Sorry, mate. Didn't mean to pry."

He dismissed my apology with a brief wave of the hand, eyes staring pensively across the deserted room. "There were four of us sharing a pokey little bedroom situated at the top of the stairs. No windows, carpets or heat, just a bed pushed against a wall covered in mould. I remember the strong smell of urine drifting up from the bedclothes as we huddled together, dreading the sound of a key rattling in the front door. We used to pray he'd fall under a bus or just drop dead, anything to keep him away."

"Was this every night?"

"Not every night. Trouble is, we never knew when, that was the worst part, not knowing. Even ten years on, the sound still haunts me, except now I don't shake so much or wet the bed."

An attempted smile failed to remove the grim expression and you just knew the story wasn't over.

"I can still see the door bursting open and hear the whimpering as he dragged one of us away. After a while you learnt to shut yourselves off from the pain and humiliation. Even the struggling became futile, so you just went quietly and let him get on with it. If you were lucky the ordeal ended in a couple of minutes, at other times you had to..."

I waited but he didn't go in to detail, not yet ready to reveal the more sordid parts of his nightmare.

"But you did get away from there?"

The question proved largely academic otherwise he wouldn't be here - not that Fireman Farley cared one way or another. He was back at 147 Longton Mews reliving the experience.

"One night, me and this other kid, a tousle-haired cockney with spindly legs and a withered right hand, hid at the top of the stairs, knowing the front door would be left unlocked while he came up to select his prey. This gave us the opportunity to escape. We had no idea where, but that didn't matter. For over an hour we hid behind an old forgotten trunk, shaking with fear as the minutes ticked away. Suddenly the unmistakable sound of a key scraping in the lock forced us further back into a corner, clinging tightly to one another as he began to climb the steep flight of stairs. Every few steps he would stop and curse, puffing like an old steam engine as he undid the leather belt ready to tan our bare arses. The indignity of it all didn't bother us ... just the pain and feel of those one inch wide weals that would take a week to heal.

"I can picture him now, swaying slightly as he wiped his brow before discharging a thunderous fart loud enough to send the other kid scurrying back into the bedroom, leaving me to face him alone. The evil in his eyes left me in no doubt as to the consequences if I remained, leaving no alternative but to make a dash for freedom. His clumsy attempt to block my way only made me more determined. The next thing I knew his fat, smelly body was falling backwards. I remember thinking how easy it was as I watched him roll over and over, coming to rest against the door, one bloodstained leg poking grotesquely through the shattered glass. I was still there when the ambulance men came to remove the body. We were never really questioned - but I'm sure the police knew.

"Shortly after, I went to live with a foster family. The other kids didn't like me because of my colour and reluctance to mix. Even the parents found my mood swings difficult to cope with … but at least they persevered, treating me with a kindness I'd never known before. I remained there for about six years by which time I had a job and a place of my own … if that's what you call an attic room, freezing in the summer, sweltering during winter and a bathroom shared by two dozen residents."

Other than narrating a school play on the works of William Shakespeare, Leroy's only other lengthy contribution to speechmaking concerned his application to join the London Fire Brigade, where he had to explain in great detail the procedure for evacuating the capital in the event of a nuclear attack. With a five year gap in between, the next speech wasn't expected until the mid-sixties - although he still hadn't finished with this one. "I've never really had a home, Joe, not one of my own, just somewhere to stay like now. Same with people. After a bad experience you become a loner, mainly because you don't trust anyone. Makes it hard to develop any kind of friendship."

"You've got friends now," I reminded him. "I know they can be a pain in the arse, especially Stan and Jock." I gave the others further consideration. "Not to mention Timex. But when the chips are down they'll back you up so you don't have to feel alone."

His eyes remained troubled; maybe they always would be. "I've never mentioned this to anyone, Joe."

I saved him the embarrassment of having to ask. "Don't worry, mate, I won't say anything although I'm sure they'd understand. Took a lot of nerve to do what you did."

"Nerve didn't come in to it - only fear."

"Whatever it was, you did the right thing. Just think of how many other kids you saved. He might still be doing it now if you hadn't come along. Bastards like him shouldn't be allowed to live, so don't feel guilty about it. Left to me, you'd get a bloody medal."

"I don't know about that, Joe! It was murder whichever way you look at it … well manslaughter anyway."

"I'm beginning to know exactly how you feel, mate."

"Why, have you murdered anyone?"

My delayed response followed the return of Stanley Clark, whistling *The Happy Wanderer*. "No, not yet … but it's only a matter of time."

Chapter 13

The wind blew straight down from the Arctic, penetrating our coarse uniforms with enough force to produce a succession of shivers and muffled expletives. Even the fast-moving rain clouds joined in as they followed our laboured progress towards the rifle range, determined to make the next two hours even more of a test.

Captain Yates watched our approach with a mixture of apprehension and fear. Ten years instructing recruits in the use of firearms had left him minus two fingers and a right earlobe. Having somehow managed to avoid the maze of bombs, mines and booby traps at El Alamein in 1942 without so much as a scratch, he then had the ill-fortune to be shot fifteen years later by a short sighted national service lad who completely misread the instructions - 'fire when I nod my head.'

Calmness and integrity, two of the qualities most officers had in abundance, were never mentioned in any of the captain's assessments. In fact, one instructor remarked 'his use of foul and abusive language went beyond the rules of acceptability and should be curtailed.'

Every new intake fired him with a determination to remain calm and in control - a position he had yet to maintain longer than twenty minutes without resorting to his favourite form of punishment which earned him the title of Big Chief Running-on-the-Spot.

"Alright, men! For your first lesson I'm going to explain the workings of a Lee Enfield rifle … how to strip it down, fire it and reassemble."

The sequence failed to impress a smirking recruit who immediately pointed out the difficulty in firing a stripped down rifle.

Captain Yates satisfied himself with a long drawn-out glare before demonstrating his skills with two of the tasks, only to discover its main function wouldn't operate.

Fortunately, a young Brummie, fresh from a successful apprenticeship at the BSA Armaments Factory, pinpointed the fault. "There's no firing pin, sir."

With his authority undermined and his knowledge brought into question, the captain's chances of remaining calm wavered between slim and hopeless and resulted in the first demonstration of running-on-the-spot. While the Birmingham lad bounced angrily up and down, the rest of us tackled the firing range, still partly shrouded by a fine, damp mist. At a distance of one hundred yards, the ten foot high replica of a grim-faced soldier proved an elusive target - in fact, quite a number couldn't even see it.

"Where is it?" enquired a puzzled gunner staring in the wrong direction. His mate scanned the horizon from left to right and then back again, one eye closed, right arm bent out of sight. "I see no ships, only hardships. Kiss me, Hardy."

The impersonation failed to improve the officer's fragile temperament and, in no time at all, Admiral Nelson joined the apprentice. At eighty yards from the prone position our aim improved, but not enough to prevent Captain Yates from demonstrating his skills from standing and kneeling positions.

"That's how it's done. No reason you can't all do the same." He fingered the missing earlobe, pausing as if trying to recall how he lost it. "You're no good to the army if you can't shoot."

"Did he say shoot or shit?" whispered a voice from behind steel-rimmed spectacles. "Because I can't do either at the moment."

"Quiet!" boomed the captain, shielding his eyes as he stared down the firing range. "Now can anyone see the next target?"

"Yes sir." volunteered Stan, moving alongside the officer. "It's straight ahead of you, just to the left of those trees." He confirmed the position with an outstretched arm. "Can you see it now, sir?"

The captain knocked his arm away. "Of course I can see it, you stupid bastard ... I put the bloody things up."

We stood around while Stan ran-on-the-spot, face changing from pale to red and finally crimson.

At times like this, Horace Yates questioned the wisdom of punishing young, trigger-happy gunners when they were issued with live ammunition a few minutes later.

"Now is there anyone else who can't see the target?"

The few who raised their hands were hopeful an eye examination may reveal some form of defect, thus shortening their national service to an acceptable five or six weeks - except the captain wasn't interested. He was already walking away, hoping for better results at the sixty yard marker.

"This time I want you to think of these targets as advancing German soldiers and blast the bastards to bits." His voice jumped two octaves. "Repeat after me. The only good German is a dead German."

Much to his surprise, very few joined in. "Come on, don't just stand there. You'll be fighting the buggers one day. I had to, so did my father, now it's your turn."

A pasty-faced gunner with the unfortunate name of Ivan Hoffman caused a minor delay in our firearms education when he raised a finger with all the authority of a cricket umpire signalling a run. "Why sir? We're not at war."

Captain Yates could sit all day holding a fishing rod - at peace with the world as he watched the float bobbing up and down. Even an unrewarding session failed to raise his blood pressure. Conversely, just ten minutes on the rifle range with some of the idiots he had to contend with caused it to soar well beyond the danger limit. "How do you know we're not at fucking war?"

"There's been nothing in the papers about it, sir."

The captain removed his hat and studied it from every angle before deciding it was his. He replaced it hurriedly. "What's your name, gunner?"

"Hoffman, sir."

Suspicion lined the officer's face, subsequently projecting itself to his voice.

"What sort of fucking name is that?"

Gunner Hoffman wasn't quite sure how to answer. "It's just a name, sir."

"It's a fucking German name, Hoffman! For all we know you could be a fucking spy, Hoffman." He glanced around for support. "We can't have people like you walking around camp ... lot of top secret equipment here, wouldn't want it to get into the wrong hands." Pointing his gun towards Hoffman's chest, he said, "Put your hands on your head and the rifle on the floor."

"Which shall I do first, sir?"

The safety catch came off the officer's thirty year old Lee Enfield, prompting a swift response from Gunner Hoffman.

"Now what shall I do, sir?"

"Why don't you shoot him, sir?" Suggested Jock, convinced it could mean an early release and not just for Gunner Hoffman. "Go on, sir -

pull the trigger."

Captain Yates, not for the first time, found himself in a predicament of his own making. "Get running-on-the-spot, gunner." A chorus of groans encouraged him to increase the punishment. "For thirty minutes."

Steve leant forward, stale breath warming my eardrums. "The man's a lunatic."

"He certainly doesn't care for Germans. I wonder who else he dislikes?"

Captain Horace Yates scanned the sea of disappointed faces and we soon found out. "Name?"

"Farley, sir."

"You ever shot anyone, Farley?"

"Not yet, sir."

Leroy commenced bobbing up and down alongside Gunner Hoffman.

Captain Yates called everyone to attention before checking his earlobe, but the end was still missing. "If the Germans are charging around raping our women are you just going to stand there?"

"No, sir!" yelled Jimmy Johnson, a five foot three Jewish boy with a nose you could swing from. "We'll join in … and then sort out the Germans."

"That's the spirit." The captain thumped his fist into an open palm, encouraged by the muffled laughter. "Knock the shit out of 'em, grind the bastards into the ground." He emphasised the threat with a glistening boot, twisting it from left to right. "What are we going to do, men?"

"Blow their bollocks off, sir."

"Kick the crap out of 'em."

"That's better men - now we're really getting angry."

"I certainly am," exclaimed an indignant Welsh voice. "My pen friend's German."

He also joined the spot runners.

We listened in disbelief as the irate officer insulted Germans, Russians, Italians, Gypsies, anyone of mixed parentage, and the bastard who nicked his fishing tackle. He stared long and hard at Leroy and decided against including the blacks. "Are you ready for battle, men?"

A lacklustre response went unnoticed as he issued further instructions in a voice somewhere between sarcastic and patronising. "Just remember you're using live ammunition so don't piss about or point it at anyone." He waited for the news to sink in before continuing. "When I give the order, I want you to run forwards in the crouched position, rifles at the ready. Any questions?"

"What if we fall over?"

Captain Yates gazed with curiosity at the bent figure of 'Lofty' Collins, whose size fourteen boots left him with the gait of a penguin. "You're only allowed to fall over if you get shot."

With a final glance at his watch he produced a silver whistle, examining both ends before deciding which should go in his mouth. "On my first whistle I want you in the ready position but don't start running until you hear the second."

The chrome instrument shone as he placed it between pursed lips and blew, pausing while a couple of stragglers tried to recall his earlier instructions. He accompanied the second whistle with a frantic waving of the arms, and then we were off.

Three dozen national servicemen ran half-heartedly across the uneven ground, yelling obscenities as they circled obstacles and leapt over man-made ditches. Suddenly a leading runner lost his footing and parted company with a rifle already free of the safety catch. He hit the damp grass with little more than a dull thud - unlike the gun which landed with a thunderous bang; a warning the rest of us to watch out for stray bullets.

Everyone, led by the captain, threw themselves to the ground and, in a matter of seconds, the range became a graveyard - until the soft whimperings of a ginger-haired gunner began to drift across the undulating surface. "Help! I've been shot. Somebody help me, please."

Mass hesitation prevailed as everyone waited for the joker to leap up, brandishing his weapon and a huge grin. When this didn't happen and another pitiful plea for assistance echoed through the mist, those nearest went to investigate, and suddenly a dozen faces were peering down at the still figure.

"Let me past." demanded the captain, shoving people aside with the butt-end of his rifle. "He's probably twisted an ankle."

"No, he's definitely been shot, sir." confirmed the first man on the scene, holding out a red hand. "Here's the blood."

"Oh, shit!" wailed the officer after inspecting the evidence. "He has been shot. Oh, bloody shit!"

A sea of faces stared down at the lifeless gunner - mouth open, eyes wide and unmoving.

"He looks dead to me," someone muttered.

"And me," confirmed another, solemnly shaking his head.

"Oh, shit!" the captain repeated, reaching for his missing earlobe. "That's just what I need ... a fucking dead soldier. I told you all not to fire until I gave the order. You're all witnesses."

"It was an accident, sir."

"Oh, yes. You try telling that to the CO. He'll blame me for this."

"Wasn't your fault, sir."

"Why didn't he get shot with one of the other officers?"

"He couldn't help it, sir."

"Of course he could. He got in the way of the fucking bullet. Have you any idea how much paperwork this will involve ... duplicate of this, triplicate of that. And there'll be an investigation. This could put my promotion back by twelve fucking months."

I leaned forward and touched the captain's sleeve. "Shouldn't we do something before it's ... too late?"

At this stage his army training appeared to have deserted him completely. "Too late." He went whiter than the victim. "What do you mean ... too late?"

"Well, he could bleed to death or even catch pneumonia."

"Oh, shit. I never thought of that."

We stared from the frightened gunner to the officer, waiting anxiously for his next move, which came with a whoop of delight. "If it was pneumonia we could say he had it before."

"That wouldn't account for the blood though, would it, sir?"

"Oh, fucking shit!"

Ginger's eyes began to flicker as he waited for death to arrive. "I'm going to die, aren't I, sir?"

The captain's silence confirmed the worst.

"How long have I got, sir? A week? A day? Five minutes?"

"Oh, shit. It may not be that serious, gunner."

A fresh face leaned forward. "I think it is, sir. You can see the whites of his eyes. My dog went like that just before he had a fit and bit the old man."

"Did you have him put down?"

"Had to, sir. The poor old sod was frothing at the mouth. The dog survived though."

Everyone moved back except the captain, anchored by the injured man's cold, clammy hand.

"Tell me the worst, sir … I can take it."

The officer shook his leg but the hand remained. "Another five years and I could retire with an unblemished record." For the first time he looked down at the prostrate gunner. "Now you've fucked that up."

"Sorry, sir."

"Unless … unless we could put it down as … attempted suicide."

"There's a good chance it could be murder," I reminded him, "if something isn't done soon."

This time he got rid of the hand with a vicious kick. "Well I didn't pull the fucking trigger. I was at least twenty yards away when it happened. You were all nearer than me."

The outburst evaporated as the injured man began to moan. "I think I'm going, sir."

"Oh, shit. I wish I could help you, gunner."

I gave the captain another nudge. "You could get him to hospital, sir. Might just be able to save him."

His expression of doom gave way to one of hope. "Yes, that could get me out of the shit. Might even get a commendation for saving his life. You hold on there, gunner … I'm going for help." He ran ten steps in the wrong direction and then returned, indicating towards the motionless body. "Who the fucking hell is he, anyway?"

"Gunner Webster, D troop."

Captain Yates set off again, leaving the rest of us staring - a mixture of sadness and pity as we waited for him to slip into unconsciousness.

"It's only a flesh wound." Leroy completed his examination, pulling a blood-stained trouser leg out of the way. "That's all it is, a flesh wound - lucky bugger!"

"Lucky!" screeched Ginger, propping himself up on one arm. "I might never walk again - I could even end up in a wheelchair."

"At least you won't have to do any marches." A note of jealousy appeared in the speaker's voice. "It's almost worth getting shot for."

I knelt down for a closer look. "You might even be declared unfit for duty - and you know what that means."

The prospect of no more national service reduced the pain considerably. "Do you really think so?"

"It's a racing certainty, mate - wounded in action."

"Wounded in action." He made it sound like a dream come true.

"That means... honourable discharge. Bloody hell!"

"And there's bound to be a pension, the sort that increases every year. Might even be able to pass it in to the kids … after all, you were fighting the Germans."

In a matter of minutes he was a new man, unable to believe his rare stroke of luck. "Good God! A pension. I wasn't going to get married … now I'm not so sure." He sat upright, ignoring the bloodstains. "I wonder if there's a chance... of a medal?"

"Don't see why not," agreed Stan. "Look how many Audie Murphy got for killing the bastards."

A Land Rover bounced to within three yards before the driver managed to locate the right pedal. Captain Yates clambered anxiously from the passenger seat. "How is he?"

I stepped forward, shaking my head with the finality of a doctor informing his patient of a terminal illness. "Delirious, sir. Rambling on about medals and pensions."

"Oh, fucking hell! Better get him to hospital before his mind goes altogether."

A dozen hands carried the injured gunner to the waiting vehicle, closely followed by the troubled officer, mentally rehearsing his plea of innocence for the court-martial. The ginger-haired gunner disappeared from sight, eyes staring dreamily into space. He was already at Buckingham Palace kneeling before the Queen.

As the morning advanced, the temperature began to rise, reducing the chill factor outside the billet and the optimism inside. The dulling monotony of army life inevitably took over.

"When do you think the bombardier's going to start us running, Joe?" The Welshman's general outlook, even his voice lacked the enthusiasm of those first few days as he succumbed more and more to the mounting pressures.

"Don't worry about it, mate. He's all piss and wind. Can you imagine him trying to run five miles a day. He's in worse condition than we are."

Timex turned away - nothing short of repatriation back to Swansea would bring a smile to his face, though a letter from Wendy might have helped.

"Which one of you is Tramp?" The questioner exhaled a cloud of smoke and waited by the door.

With a suspicion developed by the army, I raised a cautious arm towards a nervous looking soldier, trying to remain inconspicuous behind another hurried puff of cigarette smoke. "I am."

Gunner Drew stepped forward, coughing slightly through the hazy atmosphere. "The CO's wife wants to see you." Having delivered the order, Gunner Drew attacked the glowing cigarette once more, pausing prior to deliberately flicking ash on the floor. "Right away!" he barked in a voice that would have made Sergeant-Major Rhodes a proud man.

The messenger's act of bravado began to melt as six pairs of eyes settled on the tiny grey flakes covering the polished floor, and, with another nervous cough, he backed out of the room.

"You jammy bugger. I wish she'd send for me."

Jock draped a towel over his knee, hoping fifteen minutes vigorous boot rubbing would take his mind away from Mrs Carter. The memory of her revealing pose on the landing had to be relived at least three times a week, much to the annoyance of Steve, who threatened to report him for committing an indecent act in a public place. Jock claimed it kept him sane and suggested group participation, with a prize awarded to the quickest.

"If she's still frustrated, tell her she can have some of this." The Scotsman dropped both hands to his groin, holding it in a gesture familiar to us all. "I'll make her bloody eyes water."

I smiled, not wishing to discuss my intimate moments with the CO's wife - at least not until I came back.

Mrs. Carter answered the door almost immediately, black velvet housecoat buttoned from top to bottom, no make-up and the kind of expression reserved for unexpected callers. "Oh, it's you."

Any thoughts of a witty reply disappeared as she retreated inside, making it clear I was here to do a job - not exchange pleasantries. "Right, I'll leave you to get on with it."

She ushered me into the spare room, stepping aside to allow me through. The smell of recently washed hair filled my nostrils as I tentatively edged past. Even without turning I knew she would be frowning, not at me, but at life in general, which hadn't lived up to her earlier expectations when, as plain Marlene Jones from the Rhondda Valley, she had set out to join the upper class only to discover it was just as cold and lonely.

The cumbersome woollen carpet taxed my muscles for nearly an hour before it finally surrendered, held in place by a box of one and a quarter inch tacks. After stretching my aching back and performing a couple of body building poses in front of the full-length mirrored wardrobes, I moved across to the window, comparing the peace and tranquillity with the hustle and bustle of the billet. Fallen leaves still glistened from the earlier downpour and littered the sloping rear garden, leaving surrounding trees and shrubs bare and colourless.

With a sigh of regret I decided to depart, knowing I would need to prepare myself for the barrage of questions that were bound to greet my return - none of which would refer to carpet fitting.

"That looks better." Mrs Carter's face appeared around the door, newly applied lipstick contrasting sharply with two rows of perfectly even white teeth. "Why don't you go into the lounge? I'll make you a coffee."

It sounded like a chore so I declined. "No, it's okay. Thanks anyway."

"Please - it's the least I can do."

Now it was my turn to be offhand, accepting the invitation with all the enthusiasm of someone waiting to have a tooth extracted. "Okay."

I made myself comfortable in a large easy chair with well-worn upholstery supported by extra cushions and arm covers. The matching footstool remained a tempting proposition but not while I was wearing size ten boots. It reminded me of home - except Ma didn't have the curves to fill a housecoat the way Mrs Carter did.

"Here's your coffee. Be careful though, it's very, very hot."

I removed a large steaming mug from the tray, resting it hastily on the armrest as she positioned herself opposite, housecoat now partly unbuttoned revealing the full length of her much lusted after thighs.

I began to sweat, resisting the inclination to lower my eyes, even at the prospect of what lay beneath the velvet covering. In my eagerness to escape her unwavering gaze I decided to finish the drink and leave, ignoring her earlier warning until the scalding coffee hit the back of my throat, cauterising everything in its path. With great difficulty I some- how managed to contain a scream but my facial contortions more than made up for the lack of noise.

"Are you alright?," she asked. "You've gone a very funny colour."

I gave an unconvincing nod. My eyes watered as I contemplated a non-speaking existence combined with a diet of sloppy food.

Mrs Carter leaned forward, exposing her cleavage and concern as she handed me a tissue. "Are you sure there's nothing I can do? You look very distressed."

I dabbed at my eyes until the tissue became a soggy lump - hardly the way Alan Ladd would behave - he never shed tears even with a bullet in his chest. "I should be alright in a minute." I searched for a reason which could explain my woeful appearance - one she would understand and sympathise with. "It's just that I had some ... some bad news this morning."

Much to my surprise, she came over and knelt before me, her cleavage even more revealing as it blocked my line of vision. "Has someone been taken ill?"

"Er ... worse than that." My hasty reply didn't leave me with many options. "They're ... dead!"

"Oh, God! No. I never realised. You should have said." She prised my hands away, producing a small scented hanky to dab the dried tears. "Perhaps it will help if you could talk about it."

"I wouldn't know where to start." She didn't realise how true that was. "Anyway you probably have enough troubles of your own without listening to mine."

The hanky moved to my forehead. "I may be the CO's wife but I can still feel compassion ... even for a gunner." A well-manicured hand settled on my knee. "Now come on, tell me all about it."

When I couldn't think of anything to say, I gave a couple of heart-rending sobs, burying my head deep into her shoulder. I felt her stiffen but not for long, and then she began to cuddle me like a child, rocking slowly backwards and forwards. "Is it ... one of your parents?"

"My father."

"Oh, no. How awful for you. I am sorry. Was it sudden?"

"It was for him."

"What will you do?"

"I don't know." I gave an exaggerated shudder - calling on all my acting skills to inject a note of despair. "There's no one I can really talk to. Sergeant Jenkins doesn't understand because he's never had parents."

"You can talk to me." Her grip tightened around my neck and I wondered if she'd ever wrestled. "I know what it means to lose someone close and the importance of being able to discuss it. I just wish there was something more I could do."

I soon discovered the further I leant back, the further forward she came. In no time at all, Mrs Carter, wife of the CO and comforter of young gunners was entrapped on my lap. The move took her by surprise, threatening to disrupt the slow but steady progress so I played my trump card. "Oh, God! I'm an orphan."

The slow rocking movement began again, combined with a sympathetic shaking of the head. "My poor little soldier boy ... how awful for you."

I manoeuvred to a more accessible position, sliding a tentative hand inside the warm housecoat. The touch of soft, bare flesh sent shivers throughout my body.

"Oh, you're trembling, it must be the reaction - hold on tight, you'll soon feel better."

My hand found her well-rounded breast, the reaction caused us both to gasp, for very different reasons.

"You feel so... warm and comforting."

Marlene Carter tensed, remembering similar sensations from her early school days, when every boy in the class became obsessed with her eye-catching tits. She always acted indignant, pushing their grubby little hands away, but her nipples told a different story, tingling with excitement as they became conspicuous beneath the thin white blouse. "I'm not sure you should be doing this."

The objection lacked any real conviction, encouraging me to take further liberties, moving my head from the comfort of her neck, sliding slowly upwards until our lips met. There were no moves to escape, just a faint moan as my fingers brought the nipples alive, fondling each one in turn before they began to descend over a taut midriff, the smoothness giving way to the bristly triangle of newly-trimmed hair. I waited for the legs to part but they remained welded together then suddenly her hand clamped firmly on mine.

"Please don't, it isn't fair."

I immediately pulled back, displaying an expression of guilt and surprise. "I'm sorry, I didn't realise. It just felt so ... natural."

She remained flushed, breathing heavily as both hands clung to the housecoat for protection. "Things simply got a little out of hand."

I moved away, knowing I'd been too eager. "It was my fault."

"We were both to blame." Her expression softened as she recalled the feel of my hands and the mounting excitement - the missing ingredient in her sham of a marriage, but the moment had passed. "I think it would be a mistake. I'm the CO's wife, and you're just ... passing through. Another week and you'll forget all about me."

I considered the advantages of becoming a regular soldier but signing on for twenty-one years did seem a little drastic and I still may not get my leg over. "I shan't forget your kindness. And if there's anything I can ever do." When her eyebrows rose I decided to clarify the offer. "I mean as a ... friend."

We both understood, careful not to touch as we said goodbye. And then she was gone, leaving me a mixture of sadness and frustration as I headed back to the billet, knowing I would need to concoct a story that would impress every one but me.

Chapter 14

Gunner Thomas sat dejectedly on the side of his bed, mentally torturing himself with thoughts of Wendy. What she was doing and, more painfully, who she was doing it with. On days like these he cast an air of gloom over the whole billet, never for a moment considering the rest of us may also have doubts and fears.

Steve, for example, abhorred all forms of violence and intimidation and yet he belonged to an institution which thrived on bullying, worshipped bullshit, and presented killing as a worthwhile occupation.

Leroy's problem centred on the colour of his skin which bothered him more than it did us. He also had a built-in mistrust of people making it extremely difficult to develop any kind of close relationship.

Jock on the other hand covered his fears with an aggressive attitude - hardly the way to win friends and influence people. Steve called him thick-skinned but there were times when even he struggled to maintain a tough, *couldn't give a shit* image - although he would never admit it.

Stan felt inferior over most things - his job, the George Formby voice, lack of any sporting ability, and a face previously compared to a bulldog with a red hot poker up his arse. With so many complexes, he found great satisfaction living in a world of make-believe where he could dream of becoming the next Errol Flynn, whilst saving the world from destruction.

Having played Jack-the-lad for so long, I now had to live the part, giving the impression of an insensitive, sarcastic joker, with very little depth or compassion. This masquerade hid the emotions that could so easily be exposed by beautiful music, thoughts of my father or the mindless killing of wildlife. At times I even despaired for the human race, as it continued to destroy itself in the pursuit of greed.

Before I could depress myself even more, or continue with further character assassinations, the door burst open. Captain Fosdyke no longer felt the need to issue orders - expecting everyone to be prepared at all times.

Our swift response, confined to standing upright without smirking or falling over, produced a satisfied nod from the officer, looking far more composed than during our last meeting.

"Well done, excellent turnout." He ventured further into the room, determined to maintain his policy of treating everyone as equal even though he didn't really believe they were - a principal instilled by his military ancestors who thought ordinary soldiers were a different species, fit only as gun fodder or for mine detecting.

"Now if I could have your attention for a few minutes." When he smiled we began to relax. "Tonight you're all invited to a party."

"What's the catch?" Jock's suspicions reflected everyone's feelings with the exception of Stan, already anticipating a night of wine, women and song.

"Is it fancy dress, sir?"

"It is when you fucking go out." reminded the Scotsman.

Captain Fosdyke settled for a warning glance, not yet ready to exert his authority - contrary to the recommendations of officer's manual. "This is a party with a difference."

"There are no women, sir?" one asked.

"No booze?" called another.

Fosdyke's confident smirk remained in position, suggesting there would be plenty of both. "You'll have to wait and see."

"Is it to welcome us, sir? A sort of get-to-know one another party?"

Captain Fosdyke's expression became almost pained at the idea. "What possible advantage would it be for an officer to meet you, Clark?"

"I don't know, sir."

"Precisely! You are invited to the party for one reason only."

"To keep the riff raff out, sir?"

"We are the fucking riff raff." whispered Jock, resisting the urge to scratch his left testicle. "We'll either be barmen or waiters."

Fosdyke confirmed his fears. "Your function will be to serve drinks and clear up afterwards." His deepening frown gave warning of further involvement. "Using discretion at all times. In other words tact and diplomacy will be your byword. You are there to serve, not observe." He always enjoyed using that quotation, it had a certain ring to it. "Report to Sergeant Bellamy in the Officer's Mess at 1900 hours ... best uniforms, hands and nails spotlessly clean. Remember you'll be waiting on people used to the highest standard of service so don't give anyone cause for complaint."

"Shouldn't this be voluntary, sir?"

"Normally it would be, yes."

Jock looked around with the assurance of someone who'd just solved the meaning of life. "Well I'm not volunteering, sir."

"Neither am I. Get some other mugs to do it."

"Nor me - that's what the regulars are for."

Within the space of ten seconds the captain received three refusals, two prepared to give it further consideration and an uncertain maybe, none of which ruffled his feathers, thanks to a course of tranquillisers and a book on positive thinking given to him by a colleague shortly before he committed suicide. "That's up to you. As I said it is usually voluntary, although you won't be keen on the alternative. The latrines in 'F' block haven't been cleaned for months."

At 1900 hours precisely we entered the Officer's Mess, an exclusive gentlemen's club with reading lamps and red leather armchairs, the kind you struggle to escape from even before you have a drink. The carpet, a rich rustic colour, had a pile deep enough to silence the heaviest boot, ensuring an undisturbed forty winks for the handful of early evening drinkers, either dreaming of past glories or tut-tutting at the unwelcome sight of six gunners, not even in formation, lumbering across the floor.

Mess Sergeant Walter Benedictine Bellamy, a large rotund figure whose position depended on his brother-in-law's ability to supply food and drink at 25% discount, rather than on any culinary skills, smiled apologetically to the horrified onlookers as he ushered us away. "You'll get me shot coming in this way - now get into the fucking kitchen!"

The reprimand continued behind closed doors, emphasised with the assistance of a long-handled soup ladle, slicing through the air at the end of each sentence. "Any more cock-ups and you're all dead." The ladle brought down a line of tea towels drying above the hot ovens. "Oh, fuck it!" He kicked them angrily away before proceeding to outline our duties - mainly ensuring everyone had a full, clean glass, with the emphasis on clean. "We don't want any bugger complaining of lipstick on their drink, do we?"

In between serving and washing, we were to stand perfectly still in an unobtrusive position, avoiding eye contact or any form of conversation. I sidled up behind the fidgeting Scotsman. "Better keep your hands where we can see them. I don't think they'll be too impressed if one's fumbling about inside your trousers."

By 1955 hours we were stationed at our designated posts waiting to provide guests with either port or sherry, lined up on silver trays held at right angles from the body. Draped over the opposite arm was a white, starched napkin embroidered with the letters RA.

In ones and twos, the officers began to arrive, greeting each other with loud voices and hearty handshakes as they exchanged the latest gossip. Drinks selected ungraciously from sparkling trays would soon loosen their inhibitions, encouraging them to behave in a manner the rest of us would find embarrassing.

While most of us found the whole thing humiliating, Stan positively glowed with enthusiasm, abandoning his post in order to create a good impression by strolling around handing out drinks with all the finesse of a cloth-capped pensioner feeding his pigeons. As each tray emptied, we returned to the kitchen for refills, supervised by Sergeant Bellamy, growing more and more unsteady as a combination of beer, spirits and two glasses of liquid paraffin taken to relieve constipation, began to take effect.

"You buggers will never make waiters."

"We didn't come here to be waiters."

"Then you shouldn't have volunteered, now get back to fucking work." He hurried away leaving a pungent reminder as to the direction.

"Dirty sod!" muttered Jock, wafting the air with a napkin. "I'd sooner be out there serving drinks."

Timex and I remained behind, hands immersed in a sink of hot water, rinsing, inspecting and then rinsing again before stacking the glasses upside down ready for collection.

"I could do with popping back home, Joe."

"You make it sound as though you've left the gas on."

"If I could just see her for just ten minutes ... I'm sure we could work it out."

"I thought she wouldn't talk to you."

"That's only on the phone."

"My Gran's exactly the same. They frighten her to death. Do you know she still isn't sure which end to..."

"This is important, Joe. If I could only see her face to face." Stan's timely intervention sent the Welshman scurrying away, rather than risk further provocation.

"What's up with him, he's got a face like a wet weekend."

"Oh, he's just missing his girlfriend."

"He's not the only one."

"I didn't think you knew his girlfriend."

"I don't."

"Well some bugger's seeing her."

"It's not bloody me!" yelled Stan indignantly, anxious to justify his innocence. "I don't even know where she lives."

He stormed off, giving no indication why he came in.

"What's wrong with him?" Leroy deposited a tray full of dirty glasses. "He's got a face like..."

"A wet weekend, yes I know. How are things out yonder?"

"Disintegrating before your very eyes." His Arthur Askey impression failed to earn an encore – mainly due to the lack of similarity in appearance - Leroy being at least a foot taller, black and without the need to wear spectacles.

"Don't give up your day job, mate."

"I already have." He dabbed his glistening brow with a napkin before carefully restocking his tray. "And to think we have to salute these bastards."

At 2100 hours we were banished to the kitchen, spared the ordeal of speeches and presentations followed by the customary toasts, including one to the regimental goat before he was replaced by a corgi with royal connections.

Sergeant Bellamy sprawled his bulk over two chairs, no longer interested in all the razzmatazz. Having heard it all before he preferred to blot out the occasion with yet another double whisky - courtesy of the Officer's Mess.

Drink either left him poetically ecstatic, leading to a dramatic interpretation of Rudyard Kipling's *Barrack-Room Ballads*, or sullen and ill-tempered, as he reflected on a lifetime of failure. Separation, poor health and financial problems could all be blamed on the army. His estranged wife, tired of following him around the world, gave an ultimatum, confident she had more to offer than the military. After weighing up the benefits, he decided to sign on for another fifteen years - she changed the locks and bought an Alsatian. Living as a single man he neglected his health and financial commitments and was soon five stone overweight and bankrupt - drinking one and a half bottles of someone else's whisky every day.

Sergeant W B Bellamy made an effort to stand as the National Anthem reverberated into the kitchen but neither his legs nor a drinks trolley could support the weight of an eighteen stone man desperately trying to avoid doing the splits.

"Ouch!" Grimaced Steve as the last glass rolled to a standstill "I bet that made his eyes water."

I leaned forward to assess the extent of any damage. "I don't think he'll perform Swan Lake again."

"What are we going to do with him, Joe?"

"Leave him to sleep it off but we'll push him out of the way before someone trips up."

Three left feet and one right slowly moved 250lb of blubber across the tiled floor, coming to rest in a six by eight wine store, cool enough to maintain the well-stocked shelves at an even temperature. As a final act of dignity, Stan gingerly closed the sergeant's legs. "Shouldn't we cover him up, Joe?"

"Not unless he's dead."

"How can you tell?" enquired Timex, searching for signs of life.

"Usually they stop replying to letters and answering the phone."

"Bastard!" he mumbled, turning away to consider the possibility - but only briefly. Wendy rarely suffered health problems other than recurring bouts of hay fever, limiting their summertime activities but very little else. He decided death from excessive sneezing would be unusual and dismissed the idea with a two-finger salute in my direction.

No one appeared in a hurry to serve further drinks, particularly Jock, preferring to demonstrate his bottle spinning skills with one hand while the other delved deep inside his khaki trousers. "Ah! I've been dying to do that all night."

"How revolting." exclaimed Steve, screwing his nose up as the door flung open.

"Where's the mess sergeant?" Captain Bonell stood in the doorway, a dapper little man, patch over one eye and a spindly moustache. His claim to French aristocracy could only be traced to a Cornish trawler man caught fishing off the coast of Brittany. "I'm waiting!" he barked.

Only the bottle continued to move, attracting everyone's attention as it spun slower and slower, coming to rest in perfect alignment with the officer's stomach. He moved to the side recalling a similar situation at a bottle party when he actually ended up with his own wife. "Well, does anyone know where he is?"

Only Stan showed any inclination to respond, eyes flitting anxiously towards the wine store. "I think he's buggered off, sir."

"Has he, by jove." The authority left his face, replaced by mounting excitement. "And which one's Hoff?"

Six pairs of eyes stared towards the captain, producing even more colour as he suddenly remembered the purpose of his visit. "Right, you'll just have to carry on without either of them." He backed sheepishly through the door. "Well come on. Chop, chop."

"Chop, bloody chop." mimicked Jock even before the door stopped swinging. "You know what he is, don't you?"

Everyone went about their business, preferring to serve drinks rather than listen to the Scotsman's theory concerning Captain Bonell's sexual preference.

"A bloody pufter, that's what he is."

I followed them to the big room in time to witness the antics of three well-lubricated officers, violating the rousing 'Land of my Fathers' in opposition to the pianist who stuck doggedly to a selection from 'South Pacific.' Any wrong notes could be attributed to the second lieutenant draped affectionately over his shoulder, threatening to throw up over a pair of patent leather shoes as they fought a losing battle with the pedals.

Normally I enjoyed a bit of cabaret, especially when people with high normal standards make complete pratts of themselves - although it was difficult to let yourself go when one of them was tugging at your leg.

"Take me for ... a giss ... punner."

I glanced down at the bemused face, long sandy coloured hair spilling untidily over a damp forehead giving the impression of a fallen marathon runner. "Can you repeat that in English, sir?"

The sarcasm failed to register, in common with most other things as he tried again - finally conceding to the easier option with a lazy wink. "Would you take me...for ...a wee wee."

I caught Stan's arm as he walked by. "Give me a hand with this idiot before he piddles himself."

Between us, we managed to steer him towards the gents, opening the door with his head.

"Now what?" Stan's face summed up his embarrassment at having to manhandle one of Her Majesty's officers. "Or can we just leave him here."

"Not really. I doubt it he can even stand. Now let's see." I shuffled into a better position, the smell of Brylcream mixed with cigarettes and alcohol. "When I take the weight, you reach round for his…."

"Oh, no. I'm not messing with him."

"You don't have to mess with him - just unzip his trousers and take out his …"

"Bollocks!"

"There's no need to go that far."

"I've told you I'm not touching him." Memories of a public toilet in Wigan came flooding back. A complete stranger claiming arthritis in both hands asked for assistance. He still had nightmares over the shame of explaining to a court of law, the reasons for committing an indecent act, as they called it, with a known sex offender. He received a stern warning from the judge and a proposition from three members of the jury. "I'll go and fetch one of the others."

"I wouldn't bother, mate. Timex won't do it in case Wendy finds out. Steve can't in case the police find out. And Jock may refuse to let go."

As a compromise we unbuttoned his trousers, allowing them to fall before propping his half-naked body against the white porcelain. We moved nimbly back as a sudden heave emptied the contents of his stomach over the floor, reducing his chance of rejoining the party or even remaining upright. The end came with a sickening thud as hands, elbows and chest sank into the multi-coloured vomit. For long agonising seconds he somehow managed to keep his face off the floor until that too disappeared in a sea of carrots and peas, leaving only a bare, white arse pointing obscenely upwards.

"We can't leave him like this." Stan tried to think why. "It's er… undignified."

"The whole bloody night's been undignified. Having second thoughts about becoming an officer."

Stan hadn't even considered the possibility but maybe others had. "I'll probably stick with the enlisted men. That's what Elvis Presley did."

"That's a relief," I reminded him without saying who for. "Give someone else a chance. Now what are we going to do with him? People can drown in half-an-inch of water you know."

The ex-postman wasn't really listening, toying with the sound of

Lieutenant, or even Captain, Clark. This time next year he could be one of them but first he had to solve this little problem. "I think we should drag him to safety. After all, he is an officer."

Before we could launch a rescue mission, Captain Bonell appeared, his eagerness to empty a full bladder temporarily forgotten as he spotted the recumbent figure.

"I say, this looks like an interesting game." His good eye began to twinkle as he tugged excitedly on the moustache. "Can anyone join in?"

We beat a hasty retreat as the captain approached his unfortunate victim, unable to believe this rare stroke of luck.

"I'm glad to be out of there." Stan closed the door with a sigh of relief. "Let the captain see to him."

"He's probably doing that right now."

"At least he can't do much damage - not with one eye."

I was still trying to work out Stan's logic as Timex beckoned us over.

"Where've you pair been? It's like a madhouse in here. Steve's been accosted, Leroy's been insulted on a number of occasions, while Jock's threatening to duff the next person who yells, 'come on, chop, chop'. What are we going to do, Joe?"

"Clear off. We've done our job. Anyway no-one's going to miss us … they're all too drunk." I began sorting through the bottles. "Well don't just stand there, get some of these in your pockets … come on, chop, chop."

Jock clearly wasn't in a humorous mood, pissed off at having to bow and scrape for what he described as fucking parasites living the life of Old Riley. "Don't start that bloody, chop, chop crap with me. I'm up to here with chop fucking chop."

"Alright, mate. Calm down." I held out two bottles of sherry as a peace offering. "Put these in your pockets."

The Scotsman half expected someone else to wind him up but they were all busy apart from Steve.

"We can't take these. It's stealing."

"Not really," reminded Leroy. "I bet we pay for this lot out of barrack room damages."

Steve's objections failed to halt the pilfering. But Captain Jones' unexpected appearance brought everyone to a standstill. The CO's adjutant, a tall angular man with deep set eyes and a nose broken by a cricket ball, sensed something amiss but seven large rums mixed with a bottle of the finest claret greatly affected his powers of observation. "I want a word with you buggers."

The seconds ticked by as we waited, contemplating at least a severe reprimand, with the distinct possibility of six months in the notorious glasshouse.

"What do we do now, Joe?" whispered Stan, hands still poised over the bottles sticking out of each pocket.

"Just don't make any sudden moves, or he'll think you're going for your guns."

"Now I know how Gary Cooper felt when those killers came after him in *High Noon*." The menace in his eyes didn't transfer to the voice. "One move and I'll fill him full of ..."

"Whisky."

"I think we should give ourselves up." Timex regretted his involvement, unable to disguise the look of guilt. "It's not as though we're really stealing."

"Then what are we doing?" hissed Jock. "Carrying them from the table to the fridge inside our fucking uniforms?"

Steve was next to develop cold feet, knowing he would be classified as an accomplice - a charge unlikely to impress his father or make good reading on his army record. "Timex is right. If we put everything back maybe he won't say anything."

Captain Jones had no intention of saying anything, not with more important things on his mind. On the one hand, he had a duty to ensure the CO returned home safely, avoiding further embarrassing situations concerning young ladies and the regimental goat. But he had assurance from a very willing and, by all accounts, able blonde that a ride in his black Standard Vanguard, with its six-cylinder engine and 81 brake horsepower, would not go unrewarded. Alternatively, he could forget the woman, tend to the CO, and then make another attempt to relieve his frustrations on a wife he hadn't fancied since the honeymoon.

The stark choice eventually came to a conclusion with two deep intakes of breath, followed by a finger wavering between the floor and ceiling. "I want a volunteer to escort the CO safely home at midnight."

All eyes settled on me, although it was left to Jock as usual to voice their thoughts.

"You're already seeing to the wife ... may as well keep it in the family and see to the fucking husband."

Chapter 15

The frenzied earlier activities, when most of us had our first taste of kitchen duties, were soon relegated to the list of things we would never admit or include under the heading 'previous experience.' Once again, I questioned the effectiveness of national service - a doubt tonight's performance had merely strengthened. The officers were simply having a good time at great expense to the taxpayer while the rest of us would leave the army with all the skills of a chambermaid, still at the expense of the taxpayer.

The image of a highly trained fighting force led by fearless officers began to lose its glamour from day one. Admittedly discipline had improved, unfortunately, at the expense of respect - an impression confirmed as I gazed down at the untidy heap of Sergeant Bellamy, mouth wide open as he sucked in lungfuls of fresh air, expelled three seconds later with all the appeal of a toilet flushing.

I felt a mixture of sympathy and disgust standing over the beleaguered sergeant. Drink allowed him to forget his problems but they were still there when he sobered up, waiting to drag him back down again

No other organisation would tolerate such behaviour, especially when it interfered with his duties. Fortunately, the army didn't have to balance the books, or show a profit, so it could afford to employ a selection of drop-outs and misfits deficient in the normal list of employer's requirements - good time keeping, hard and conscientious work, and at least a little knowledge of the actual job.

The lads would be back in the billet by now, laughing and joking as they sampled the various bottles before tumbling into bed, giving no thought to my task of escorting the CO home. No doubt they would expect full details in the morning, something I should be able to supply with just a little imagination.

Between the hours of eleven thirty five and midnight, I discarded 27 empty bottles, rinsed 66 fluted glasses, and counted a total of 32 steps in navigating the perimeter of a kitchen expensively equipped in order to provide the widest selection of gourmet meals, in dire contrast to our limited menu.

After experimenting with different stride patterns, I eventually reduced the number of steps to 27. As if to confirm my deteriorating mental state, I repeated the process backwards, reaching 19 before a misplaced foot catapulted me on top of the comatosed sergeant - who greeted my arrival with the words 'Not now Beryl.'

Before I could extract myself, an unexpected spectator put two and two together and came up with five.

"This is turning into a bloody good party." Captain Bonell stroked each end of the moustache, and then carefully adjusted the black eye patch. "I've always fancied a threesome."

Whilst the excited officer silently congratulated himself on having the foresight to wear the latest lingerie underneath his uniform - as advertised in Kays Winter catalogue, I made a quick dash for freedom hoping Sergeant Bellamy could tell the difference between Bonell and Beryl.

With little else to do, I went in search of Colonel Carter, past the few remaining officers, whose bleary-eyed grins and hopes of sexual fulfilment would soon be erased by a long-suffering wife wearing curlers and half a jar of face cream.

The female guests had already departed, either on the arm of a young lieutenant rendered impotent by alcohol, or in the passenger seat of a senior officer's Jaguar. Both men would no doubt meet up at the MO's surgery the following morning, smiling confidently as they described another sexual marathon before admitting to the doctor that they couldn't actually remember whether they did or didn't.

I eventually led the CO across the room, reluctantly taking his elbow, the way you would assist a blind person or someone of advanced years who knows where he wants to go but can't recall how to get there. Hard to believe this was the same person who instilled fear and panic as he inspected the regiment, or read the riot act to a quivering gunner whose knife and fork were two degrees out of line.

Colonel Carter was a heavy man, maybe thirteen or fourteen stone with a bulging midriff that required something more than a cummerbund to keep it in place. His solemn countenance and stilted movements displayed the effects of too much booze but there was also a weariness about him, suggesting these monthly affairs were attended more out of duty than any desire to take advantage of the occasion.

I began to propel him along, noticing that his watery-blue eyes were staring down; unable to understand why his feet wouldn't move in a forward direction. With practice, we began to shuffle away, leaving the building behind along with the sniggers and catcalls from junior officers, fuelled by alcohol and a growing lack of respect for someone they were previously thought awesome.

So far the CO had no idea who I was, a situation I preferred to maintain as another stumble threatened to topple us both. His mumbled apology went unanswered as I struggled to keep him upright listening to the ominous rumblings emanating from beneath the over-stretched cummerbund.

We finally made it to the front door, his stranglehold on my arm dismissing any thoughts of a quick exit.

"Do you think you'll be alright now, sir?"

He braced himself against the wall, feet planted firmly apart, upper body swaying as he fumbled in the only pocket he could reach without losing balance. "There's a key here somewhere." A warning finger wavered in front of pursed lips. "Shhhhhhhh ... mustn't wake the wife."

Left with no alternative, I searched his clothes, discovering an assortment of objects before eventually locating the key.

Colonel Carter looked at me for the first time trying to understand why a complete stranger should be offering him a key. I waited for him to take over but the blank expression suggested he required further assistance.

I helped him into the well-lit hall, waiting while he re-focused before making my exit. I had no desire to meet Mrs Carter - not under these circumstances. "I think you can manage from here, sir."

When the CO failed to let go, I tried draping him over the banister, except he wasn't ready to be left.

"Would you mind ... helping me up the stairs, gunner?" Never one for throwing his weight around or bellowing orders earned Colonel Carter a reputation for remaining composed at all times. Neither the Germans nor Italians were able to ruffle his feathers, although Sergeant Jenkins succeeded on more than one occasion.

This well-decorated senior officer disliked any form of confrontation, making his wartime exploits even more incredulous. Nevertheless, he was the commanding officer and he deserved some respect - even in this condition. The winding staircase, softened by carpet, lacked the creaks and groans loud enough to alert Ma of my late arrivals home. Other than clambering through a window or sliding down chimneys, I could never prevent her from reminding me over a hot breakfast, the exact time I reached home.

The slow and laborious climb up the stairs eventually brought us within spitting distance of the landing, with a choice of at least five doors. The prospect of having to locate the correct one, take him inside and do a little undressing went far beyond the call of duty. Thoughts of placing him alongside a half-naked wife with breasts I already knew well produced more sweat than the effort of ascending fourteen steps, pulling and pushing someone whose co-operation consisted of waving an arm in the air while informing me of the virtues of marriage. Perhaps Mrs Carter had other ideas, and would invite me into bed when her husband inevitably passed out.

Two steps away from the landing, Colonel Carter gently patted my hand, his way of issuing thanks, terminating the need for further assistance. He looked a sad, lonely figure hauling himself up the last few steps, each one threatening to send him tumbling backwards into my arms.

At least he had the satisfaction of climbing into a warm bed, beside an even warmer body, longing to be kissed and caressed, though, sadly, not by him. I would be sleeping amidst smelly, unwashed bodies raging with hormones that would erupt without warning - although a soft moan often gave it away. Jock always shared his nocturnal experiences unlike Steve who denied it ever happened yet still felt the need to rinse his pyjama trousers every other morning.

Colonel Carter hesitated after pushing open one of the bedroom doors, either unsure of the reception or temporarily blinded as he shielded his eyes from the bright light. I even considered hanging about, hoping she would sense my presence and invite me in. But you never know, where women are concerned. She could just as easily scream for help and have me arrested as an intruder.

With a shrug of indifference, I descended the stairs, pausing in the hall to admire portraits of Colonel Carter's impressive heritage. I gained a certain satisfaction from reminding myself there would be no further generations of Carter's - at least not sired by him. I couldn't imagine she would have any problems in that department.

A decision regarding the hall light caused a twenty seconds delay, otherwise I would have been well away from the house before raised voices pricked up my ears. Curiosity soon overcame any concerns about eavesdropping and I was tempted to discover what really went on behind closed doors.

"You bastard! And how long has this been going on?"

I leaned forward, suddenly more alert as the same voice continued. "Fifteen years I've had to put up with you, turning a blind eye while you ran your little rackets, disrupting the whole camp and making me a laughing stock. As if that wasn't enough you then do this across me"

The CO's articulate voice, loud and clear, displayed no sign of drink as he continued the tongue lashing until you could almost feel the tension rising.

I returned to the stairs, ready to make a hasty intervention should the situation escalate, which it did, but not in the way I imagined.

"And what are you going to do about it? Throw me out? You haven't got the bloody guts, never did have. War hero! Don't make me laugh." The voice was unmistakable, even the sarcasm and threats were no surprise - Sergeant Jenkins spoke to most people that way.

"You had all the glory, promotion, and what did I get? Fuck all!"

"I put my neck on the line for you, even destroying complaints from other officers, sick of your disruptive influence, and this is how you repay me."

Even in a personal confrontation, Colonel Carter still retained a degree of control Sergeant Jenkins could never quite manage.

"Well some bugger had to keep her satisfied, you never could. Ask your wife."

I assumed the sobbing noises came from Mrs Carter, making her explanation difficult to hear. "It wasn't like that. He never gave me a choice. He said if I objected or told anyone he would expose you. I couldn't bear to see you go through that."

Colonel Carter's lengthy pause gave every indication the revelations were not only a complete shock but also believable. "How long's this been going on behind my back?"

I had no way of knowing who the question was directed at until Sergeant Jenkins replied, unable to hide his contempt for the commanding officer. "Long enough for me to get used to it. I'm amazed you've only just found out. But then you always were fucking gullible."

"Well, you know what they say. The husband's always the last to know." Colonel Carter directed the next question to his wife. "I suppose the whole camp knows about this?"

"No one knows … and they never will. Certainly not from me."

Her assurance failed to remove the doubt. "How could you let him blackmail you this way - I trusted you."

"I tried to tell you over and over again but you wouldn't listen … always defending him."

"Not any more … those days are finished, and so are you, Jenkins."

An uneasy silence followed. Either the CO had conceded or run out of objections, allowing Sergeant Jenkins to take over. "And what the hell do you think you're going to do with that fucking thing?"

"Something I should have done a long time ago."

The sergeant's laugh proved a little premature as a loud shot echoed through the house, silencing all but the screams from Mrs Carter. At this point, I didn't know if anyone had been shot or simply frightened - even the victim remained unknown, although a bookmaker wouldn't give particularly good odds on Sergeant Jenkins' chances. It may even have been suicide, or perhaps the bullet had ricocheted killing all three. The permutations began to confuse me and yet I knew a serious crime had been committed - one I wanted no part of.

The realization I could easily become involved curbed my natural instinct to investigate. Raised voices and a single shot hardly constituted a call for police reinforcements.

I covered the return journey in record time, entering the billet breathing faster than Jock who was enjoying himself beneath the vertically hung blankets.

"Didn't expect to see you until the morning."

"Yes, I can see that."

"Wasn't he interested in a threesome?"

"Never stayed to find out. Just rang the bell and left him propped up against the wall. Could still be there for all I know."

"This lot went straight to bed." His hands moved furtively around beneath the sheets. "I bet you had more excitement taking the CO home."

"No I didn't … totally uneventful. The most boring twenty minutes of my life. I can't even remember it."

The Scotsman gave me a strange look, returning to his nightly ritual as I climbed wearily into bed, grateful for the silence in order to collect my thoughts.

Dawn brought its own sounds, interrupting dreams that left randy young gunners red-faced, reluctant to leave their beds until things calmed down. Jock, however, had no such inhibitions. "Do you think it's grown during the night?"

"Oh, for Christ's sake, put the bloody thing away. I'm sick of waking every morning to the sight of ... that!" Steve's annoyance hadn't diminished from day one, when the Scotsman introduced himself with the words, 'how would you like to shake hands with this?'

Long before beds were squared off and locker layouts completed to perfection, we were informed today's parades and inspections had been cancelled, due to unforeseen circumstances. The unexpected reprieve filled me with suspicion - in contrast to everyone else. They all planned to have a leisurely breakfast and then get back to bed.

"You're quiet this morning, Joe. Everything alright?"

I reassured Steve with a nod, in no mood to join the celebrations.

"Just a bit tired, mate. Late going to bed last night. Well not that late, in fact just after you." I glanced around for Jock to confirm my story, but he was already heading for the canteen. "I left the CO on his doorstep."

"He didn't invite you in then?" Steve remained apprehensive. "For a night-cap?"

"Good God, no. We never even spoke. I just left him on the doorstep."

"So you keep saying."

Leroy was the last to leave for breakfast, determined to maintain his own high standard of 'bullshit'. "Coming over the canteen, Joe?"

"No, I'm not really hungry ... always the same after a late night, not that it was too late. I simply took the CO home ... and left him on the doorstep." I turned away, conscious that I was repeating myself - again. "You carry on, mate. I'll get something later."

Normally breakfast had to be eaten in ten minutes, with the exception of days like this, when the process could take an hour - unless something important turned up.

Something did!

"There's been a murder in the camp."

Everyone expected Steve to solve it there and then. "Some poor sod's been shot."

Jock's return coincided with an itch in the usual area. "The whole place is sealed off. Fucking police everywhere. I wonder who it is."

"According to the cook, it's somebody important."

"That rules out everyone we know, then." I replied. I was almost tempted to offer an explanation until I considered the risks. "They'll soon find out who did it."

"They already know." Stan enjoyed gossip, good or bad, believing it gave him a certain standing. "The police reckon he was blown to bits by the IRA."

So the exaggerations had begun. This time tomorrow they would be looking for a serial killer with a limp, who answered to the name of Paddy.

"Stroke of luck for us, though." Steve tried to remain subdued in respect of the occasion as he pondered the possibility of early release.

"Someone always benefits from another person's misfortune."

"So long as it's us I don't give a monkeys. The sooner we're out of this shit hole the better."

Jock's ability to simplify everything, always received a look of contempt from a would-be-lawyer, trained to do just the opposite. "Don't you ever think of anyone but yourself?"

Steve turned quickly in my direction, unwilling to exchange words with anyone who exhibited violent tendencies. "Will your mother be coming down to watch you pass out, Joe?"

"No, it's too far, and there's no one to bring her. How about your parents?"

"I doubt it. They've never been interested in anything I've done before. Anyway father suffers with his ticker ... he's not supposed to get excited."

"He'll be in no danger here then."

Everyone had their own version of the shooting and who the victim might be with the exception of Steve. Assumptions were not part of his language, only facts. "I really think we should wait before making predictions, we'll know soon enough."

Little else was said or heard about the situation until mid-morning, with the unexpected appearance of Bombardier Hawkins who obviously had more on his mind than concerns over unmade beds and dishevelled gunners. "You may as well know Sergeant Jenkins was shot dead in the early hours of the morning outside Colonel Carter's home."

His long pause and searching look suggested he hadn't excluded us from the list of possible suspects. "It appears he went to ensure the CO had arrived home safely from the officer's party. The one you lot cocked up. Obviously a person, or persons, lay in waiting - for what reason we're not really sure at this stage."

Bombardier Hawkins' assessment of the case would send most detectives back to college for a further course in criminology. "According to a statement from Captain Jones, one of you escorted him home."

"I did, Bombardier."

"Tramp, I might've guessed you'd be involved." He approached in his usual menacing way. "Why you? Why not one of the others?"

At any other time my shrug would be treated as disrespect, but clearly he wasn't here for reprisals. "I'm waiting, boy."

"I've been there a couple of times." I prayed Jock wouldn't complicate matters by referring to my so-called liaison with Mrs Carter. "I know the way."

"That's another thing, Tramp. Why should the CO's wife ring to see if you're alright?"

"She's a very compassionate woman, Bombardier."

"Well I've never seen much of it. I was in hospital for six bloody months - the first day back at work she gave me a bollocking for not standing to attention."

"That sounds... reasonable."

"I was in a fucking wheelchair."

His face didn't encourage sniggers or offhand remarks so we remained silent and serious.

"I'm still not sure why you should escort the CO home. Every bugger in camp knows where he lives."

Another shrug went unpunished. "I suppose he trusts me."

"Why the fucking hell should he trust you?"

"He has to trust somebody. How else would he know what's going on?" All thoughts of Sergeant Jenkins were swept aside as his suspicions began to grow. "What do you mean - what's going on?"

"I just let him know how the new recruits were settling in. He's interested in all of his men, even you. He's always asking, what's Bombardier Hawkins up to these days."

Hawkins adopted a defensive attitude, oblivious to the captive audience. "How does he know I'm up to anything?"

"No idea, bombardier. He questions me, I don't question him."

"Some bastard's opened their big mouth."

"Well, it wasn't me."

Bombardier Hawkins had made a lot of enemies. National servicemen, regulars, and even some of the officers would be glad to see the back of him. But he didn't think any of them would go this far.

"I bet it's that bloody driver of his, always trying to drop me in the shit."

"You think he could be the one?"

"Pound to a fucking penny. He's always had it in for me ever since I got promoted and he didn't."

"I wouldn't let him get away with that, Bombardier."

His eyes narrowed and I knew the driver was in trouble. "Don't worry, his fucking days are numbered. This time tomorrow he'll be cleaning out the shithouse ... might even be doing it to-*fucking*-day."

His precision turn and measured stride pattern were not in evidence as he stormed out, planning the downfall of Gunner Morgan who would soon be swapping his driving gloves for a toilet brush and plunger.

Steve came over, furrowed brows confirming his confusion. "What was all that about?"

"Originally Sergeant Jenkins, and then he got sort of ... sidetracked."

"Funny how he picked on you, though."

"Yes, hilarious."

"Joe could be a key witness in all of this. After all, he was the last person to see Sergeant Jenkins alive, allegedly."

There were times when I admired Steve's perception but this was not one of them. "I think the murderer would be the last, mate."

I lay back on the bed and closed my eyes to deter further questions. I had enough of my own to answer. How did the body travel from upstairs to outside? What happened to the murder weapon? Who actually discovered the body? And what should I do about it?

Morally I felt obliged to provide a statement which would leave the CO facing a murder charge, unless he denied it. Mrs Carter would surely back him up and then suspicion could fall on me. I was there at the time of the shooting and yet failed to either investigate or report it. A competent barrister would soon provide a motive and my City & Guilds in machine shop engineering would hardly stand up against a highly respected war hero with an OBE and a DSM.

Further queries had to be put on hold at the sudden appearance of Captain Fosdyke, unconcerned at our lack of action and bedraggled demeanour. "Relax, gentlemen, this is purely a social call. For reasons you may already be aware of, we are dispensing with the customary passing-out parade and sending you on a week's leave."

Under the circumstances a round of applause appeared inappropriate so we confined our delight to sighs of relief mixed with silly smiles.

"Collect your passes and travel documents from the admin office."

"When can we leave, sir?"

"Right away but don't forget to report back in seven day's time. We can then decide on your next move. Any further questions?"

While everyone else prepared for a quick getaway, I sidled over to the captain. " Exactly how did Sergeant Jenkins die, sir?"

"Shot in the chest from close range by all accounts, gunner."

"Any idea who did it, sir?"

"Well, there's no doubt in my mind ... although I doubt if they'll find the killers."

I gave him a prompt before he could move on. "Who do you suspect then, sir?"

"It's obviously the IRA ... probably after arms for their pathetic crusade. Colonel Carter's most upset over the incident. He blames himself."

"Why, did he do it?"

Having done his duty, Captain Fosdyke had no wish to prolong the conversation, especially along those lines. He paused on his way out as if suddenly remembering who the killer was. "Incidentally, we discovered a pile of undelivered mail in the sergeant's room, most of it addressed to a ... Gunner Thomas. Better collect it before you leave. Good day, gentlemen."

"Bastard!" snarled Timex, not sure whether to laugh or cry. "That's no way to talk about the dead," I reminded him, but the fuming Welshman wasn't listening, concerned only with retrieving his missing post.

"What's going to happen to us, Joe?" Leroy's original dread of army life no longer warranted a quick return to the fire service. "Do you think they'll keep us together?"

"Don't see why not. We've put up with one another for the past few weeks, may as well carry on for the rest of it."

"At least there'll be no Sergeant Jenkins to muck things up for us."

"Yes, that was a real stroke of luck … some bugger shooting him." Jock's right hand made another foray into his trousers. "Now all we have to do is get rid of that bastard, Hawkins."

Steve ignored the Scotsman's crass comment, mentally preparing his case for the prosecution. "I wonder who did kill, Sergeant Jenkins."

"They appear to be blaming the IRA."

"Nonsense. Anyway where's the motive?"

No one really cared. They were more concerned with getting away before the army changed its mind - not that that prevented Steve voicing his opinion.

"Does anyone know what Sergeant Jenkins was doing outside the CO's home at midnight?"

"Could be a peeping fucking tom, for all I care."

Steve mentally removed Jock from the conversation. "He doesn't strike me as the type of person who would be concerned about others."

"Alright, smart arse - who did kill him?"

Steve chose to ignore the Scotsman, turning his attention in my direction. "What about you, Joe? Any ideas?"

My protracted silence failed to distract him.

"You were there, didn't you see or hear anything?"

Steve's way of making everyone feel guilty began to work as my voice snapped out a reply. "I've already told you. I simply left him at the front door. We didn't even speak. Anyway, what the hell's it got to do with you?"

My reaction forced him into a hasty climb down - something he would have to overcome in order to excel as a courtroom lawyer.

"Just looking for a motive, Joe."

"Well look somewhere else. I've got more important things to do." I took my anger out on the suitcase, thumping it down until he clips fell into place. This time tomorrow I would be enjoying home cooking, prior to sampling half-a-dozen pints of Banks's bitter at the Royal Oak. But the attraction of Wolverhampton diminished slightly when Timex returned with the undelivered mail, including one from Julie, asking if we could meet up again.

She would have to wait a while but at least it provided another reason for me to come back.

We said our goodbyes at Gravesend railway station, the growing bond surprising us all. Having survived twenty one years without a close friend, I now found myself saddled with five making the prospect of actually finishing national service, not only bearable but also enjoyable as we united against the common enemy.

The end